Sue,
Have fun
Amy & her story.

Pamela

Good Enough

ALSO BY PAMELA GOSSIAUX

Why Is There a Lemon in My Fruit Salad?
How to Stay Sweet When Life Turns Sour

A Kid at Heart: Becoming a Child of Our Heavenly Father

Six Steps to Successful Publication: Your Guide to Getting Published

PAMELA GOSSIAUX

Good Enough

Tri-Cat Publishing

Visit the author's website at: www.PamelaGossiaux.com

First Printing, November 2016

ISBN 978-0-9976387-3-8 (paperback)
ISBN 978-0-9976387-2-1 (ebook)

Cover Design: The Killion Group, Inc.
Editor: Erin Wolfe, WordWolfe Copy Editing
Formatting: Dallas Hodge, www.ebeetbee.com

Published in the United States by Tri-Cat Publishing.

Tri-Cat Publishing

To my friends in Writer's Group:

It takes a village to publish a book.
I'm blessed to have you in my tribe.

Chapter One

You know those dreams that you never want to end? I'm having one.

I'm at a Hawaiian luau, dancing with a strange, dark-haired man who may be my boyfriend (I can't see his face in the dream), and he's about to breathe something sweet into my ear. Then the tiki torch next to me starts my hula skirt on fire, and because I don't want the moment to end, I grab a water glass off a nearby table and try to douse it discreetly. I hear a sort of hissing, sputtering sound, and the handsome man (now looking more like Johnny Depp) asks where the steam is coming from. Before I can take that to be a romantic come-on, I realize in that half-dream sort of way it's the cat yakking up a hairball. In real life.

As I wake up, I open my left eye a tiny slit, trying to decide if my dream is preferable to my reality. And that's when my brain registers that it's daylight - *daylight* - in my room.

I sit upright and grab the clock. The alarm didn't go off, and I have ten minutes to get ready or I'll be late for work.

I scramble out of bed, grab the clothes I had set out the night before (Thank God I'm so organized!), and start pulling on my skirt. My legs are stubbly, but with no time for a shower and shave, I have to find some tan hose, quick. Maybe black hose would be better. Hmmm…No…oh dear. Eight minutes left.

I pull the rest of my clothes on and run to use the bathroom just as I hear the last "huuurrmpphhh," signaling the cat has finally rid herself of the offending hairball.

I race into the kitchen, nearly slide in the mess, and throw a paper towel over it to hide it.

"Sorry, kitty," I say, sticking a piece of bread in the toaster. "No time for clean-up now."

While the bread is toasting, I brush my teeth, add makeup to my face, and grab my purse. To save time styling my hair, I pull it back in a ponytail.

1

"Not bad," I say, surveying it in the mirror. It gives me the clean-swept businesswoman look.

Something's burning. The toast!

I run into the kitchen and grab my black toast and car keys. The cat starts meowing at an alarming level and tries to trip me as she realizes I'm not going to feed her.

"Eat dry food this morning, honey," I say. "Your tummy's too upset for canned food."

I slam the apartment door behind me, leaving Mouser in distress.

"Running a bit late, aren't you Amy?" says Mrs. Crabbs, my nosy neighbor who is in the hallway getting her morning paper.

"Yes, so can't talk now," I say. She runs her eyes up and down me and snorts in a disapproving way as I race outside.

I climb in my car, only two minutes late. I feel grimy from no shower, am not thrilled about my toast, and miss my morning coffee. To make it worse, I get behind a little old grandpa who can barely see over the wheel and is going half the speed limit.

I'm gripping the steering wheel, hunching my shoulders, and starting to feel a pounding in my temples. I begin to grumble to myself, which makes tiny toast crumbs drop down on my white blouse.

"My life stinks!" I say. Then I remember that I'm turning over a new leaf. I've been reading Myra Winnrey's book *Claiming Happiness,* and I'm on the chapter where I'm supposed to be using positive self-talk.

"Okay," I say. "I have a great life. I have this awesome job that I love."

And it's true. I'm a writer for InterFind, a huge Internet search engine. I work with very creative people and write advertising copy for our advertisers. It's a good job, it pays well, and I have a window office.

"I have the world's best boyfriend," I remind myself. This is true too. Bart is a lawyer, tall and handsome, and is the love of my life . He travels a lot helping other people who can't afford lawyers and has even done some international work. Just this week he's out of town helping those less fortunate in Haiti or some island. He'll be back this weekend, and we'll go out to dinner and—

The old man suddenly stops, and I run into his car. It's not hard enough to set off my airbag, but I was in the middle of taking a bite of toast and it crushes against my mouth, sending crumbs over the rest of me.

"Oh my gosh," I say, and jump out of the car. "Are you all right? Sir?"

He looks so old he could be dead. Maybe that's why he stopped—maybe he had a heart attack. *Oh my gosh.*

I run to his driver's side window and see that his head is bent low. My fears are confirmed—he *is* dead! Or maybe just unconscious.

I pull out my cell phone to call 911 and rap on his window. He looks up, and I see a cell phone in his hand. He's *texting.*

"What the...?"

No...I'm thinking positively. Maybe he's texting 911. Can you do that?

He rolls down his window and answers his phone, which is now ringing.

"Wait a minute, honey," he says into the phone. "The woman who hit me while we were talking is here. She looks like one of those feminists . No, I'm all right. Really. I'm sure insurance will cover it. I'll call you back."

I'm dumbfounded.

"Sister, you need to watch where you're going," says the old man.

"You stopped!" I said. "You...you were *texting* on your cell phone?"

"I was talking to my granddaughter when you hit me," he said. "She's preggers and had the ultrasound yesterday. She was telling me the sex of the baby, but you went and ruined the moment. Her grandmother is probably turning over in her grave. You ought to be ashamed of yourself. What were *you* doing? Putting makeup on? You young people are all alike—except for my Nellie."

I haven't had time yet to call 911, but a police officer pulls up then, before I have a chance to collect my thoughts. He walks slowly over to me and glances down at my fender.

3

"Any damage?" he says, only mildly interested.

Of course, there's damage! My fender has a small dent in it. I point this out to him.

"License, registration, and proof of insurance," he says.

"This is her fault!" Gramps jabs a finger at me.

"What? Wait, no, *he* was *texting*!" I say.

The officer raises an eyebrow and then goes back to his car to fill out some forms. Clearly, he was hoping for a more exciting morning. I can't help feeling offended.

I glance at my fender. It's not that bad, so I get back into my car. After a few minutes, the officer comes back and gives me a ticket for tailgating, which I assure you I was *not* doing.

"Have a nice day, ma'am." He tips his hat. I thank him (because I was raised that way) and pull out. I scowl at Gramps as I pass him. He scowls back.

"At least I have my job," I say to myself. "And now I have a ticket to explain why I'm late."

Positive self-talk.

I pull into the parking garage and walk inside, slinging my spring jacket over my chair.

"Morning, Amy," says Hack. "Boss wants to see you."

"Oh. I can explain why I'm late." I hold up my ticket, smiling. "I got in a little accident."

"Wow, dude. You okay?"

"Yeah, just a little fender bender."

Hack is cool. I work with really cool people. Hack, for example, is named such because supposedly he can hack into any computer. He dresses a bit oddly and has a ponytail longer than mine. He wears glasses, but that's where geekiness ends and strange begins. He wears bright-colored checkered shirts and Bermuda shorts with flip-flops no matter what the weather, and it gets pretty cold here in Michigan in the winter. Hack looks like a hippie surfer.

I grab a cup of coffee and head to the boss's office.

"Hi, Amy," says Andrea, his receptionist and my best friend. Andrea dyed her hair green last week for St. Patrick's Day, and it's still the color of a shamrock. She's wearing pink, because she has been trying to dress to match her hair. Brown, for example, clashes with green, she says, which I don't understand since trees are essentially green and brown. This morning she looks like a leprechaun princess.

Andrea is acting weirdly and doesn't raise her eyes. She seems to be avoiding my gaze.

"George," I nod hello to another co-worker.

"Amy, for what it's worth...well, I think you're great," he says.

George is gay and the best-dressed man I've ever met. He works on the art part of my ad copy, and we get along swell. George is...well, he's a colorful dresser too. He always wears scarves and rings and has a pair of shoes for every outfit. I would love to see his closet.

I slip into Max's office. Max is a pretty good boss. He's fun, flirty, and offers tons of rewards and incentives to us employees. Last summer he took us to a high ropes course.

"Amy," he says. "Close the door, dear."

I do and sit down in the chair across from his desk.

"I can explain why I'm late," I say. "I got in this little fender bender." I wave my ticket at him.

"Oh." Max waves his hand at me, dismissing the ticket. "I'm not worried about that."

See? I work for a really cool boss.

"Amy, you know the company has been running behind these past few months...not selling as much ad space as we'd like."

"Yes," I say.

"I'll make this as painless as possible. We have to...make some cuts. We're laying you off."

I'm too stunned to talk. We stare at each other for a few seconds in silence. Finally, I stutter,

"What? Why me? Why not...why not the ad salespeople?"

"Well, Amy, if we don't have ad salespeople, we'll sell even fewer ads, right?"

"But...I have seniority. I am...I am the *writer*."

"You do have seniority over some, Amy, and we took that into consideration. But the truth is...the truth is we're trying to figure out what we can do to make our company pop more. And you...well, you don't pop."

"What?"

"Look at how you're dressed."

I looked down at my gray skirt and white blouse. I had gone with the black hose and black shoes.

"What's wrong with my clothes?"

"Look at George," he waves his hand toward the door. "Look at Andrea. At *me*."

Max has on blue jeans, a bright red shirt, and an orange jacket with a white tie. It's loud, but it actually matches. "Look around my office."

Brightly colored paintings hang on the wall. The carpet is in different color blocks, contrasting with the white walls.

"Now look at you," he says.

I look down at my clothes again.

"I don't get it," I say.

"You don't pop," he says. "Amy, you're boring."

"You're firing me because I'm boring?" I say.

"Frankly...yes."

Max quickly tells me about my severance pay, but I hardly hear him.

I return to my desk, blinking back tears. Nobody will look at me. Did everybody know except for me?

Andrea brings me a cardboard box. There are tears in her eyes, but she doesn't say anything. I pack up my spider plant, my photos of me and my boyfriend Bart, and the small collection of cat figurines I had across the top of my computer. That's it. Five years here and that's all I've personalized my office with?

Slowly, I take my box and walk out of InterFind into the streets of Ann Arbor. I can't believe this. I have–had–the best job ever. I'm in shock. I certainly didn't see this coming.

I climb into my car, set the box on the seat next to me, and wonder what to do next. It's only 8:30 a.m. For the first time in forever, I have nothing to do on a Monday morning.

So I call my mom.

The phone rings several times. I'm starting to wonder if she's up, when she answers, out of breath.

"Mom?"

"Oh, hi, Amy. Your dad and I are speed walking."

"Where?"

"At the park. Your dad's cholesterol is up, and the doctor recommended exercise. So here we are!"

"How far have you walked?"

"Not far…we just got here. Whew! This is exhilarating!" There's lot of puffing on her end of the phone. Obviously, they're both out of shape.

"Did Dad's doctor tell you to start out slowly?" I ask.

"You know, baby steps."

"Oh, honey, you worry too much. We'll be okay—oops! Watch out, Herb! Sorry, Amy. Dad almost tripped. I don't know why they don't cut that tree branch out of there. So, honey, what was it you wanted?"

Now just didn't seem to be the time to tell her I'd lost my job.

"Nothing, Mom. I've got to go. I'll call you later."

"Okay."

"Mom?"

"Yes, dear?"

"Do you think I'm boring?"

"Oh, gracious, no!" says my mom. "Do you remember that time when we went out to that ethnic restaurant and you were the only one in our family who was brave enough to pick the food you didn't know how to pronounce? The rest of us stuck with something boring, like salad, but you went for the most foreign thing on the menu."

I remember. I also remember spending the rest of that night in the bathroom.

"Okay. Thanks, Mom."

I hang up and wonder what to do next. I'm still sitting in the parking garage.

Then my phone rings. It's Bart! Just seeing his name pop up in the caller ID window makes me feel better.

"Hi, Bart!"

"Can't talk long," Bart says. "You know, saving the world and all. But I'll be back in town today, and I want to take you out to dinner. I just need to catch a nap in the afternoon, but I can pick you up at seven."

"Ohhhh!" I say. "Where are we going?"

"Someplace special. Someplace you've wanted to go for a while."

"I'm intrigued," I say. Then I remember my awful morning, and I want to tell him about it. "It's so great to hear your voice. I've had a rough morning."

"Amy? I've got to go. Lots going on here."

"You have a really clear connection for so far away," I say.

"Hon, you're breaking up." Bart says. I hear something that sounds like the wind blowing through an open car window. Or howling winds in Haiti. "Love you! Bye!"

The line goes dead. It's strange. I almost feel like he cut me short, but Bart would never do that unless there was something really urgent he had to attend to. Bart is the most incredible boyfriend, and I feel better just having talked to him. I wish he had more time. It would have been nice to tell him about my morning. He's a great listener and always has something helpful to say. It's the lawyer in him—always trying to fix my problems. Maybe I can sue InterFind. Hmmmmm. There's an idea. Can you really fire somebody for being boring?

Bart and I met two years ago in a JavaJoes. I was picking up my morning coffee on my way to InterFind, and he was doing the same, only he was off to meet a client. I paid, turned too quickly, and there he was. My coffee splashed on him and I nearly burnt him, but we both laughed. It was like one of those meetings you see in a romantic comedy. We just clicked, and he asked me out to dinner that same night. We've been seeing each other ever since.

Actually...today's our two-year anniversary. It suddenly hits me. He's taking us out for our anniversary! And to someplace special! I feel my heart start pounding with excitement.

Then I gasp because it occurs to me: I bet he's going to propose. I swallow, my mouth suddenly dry from the excitement. That's it! He's taking me out to someplace special to propose to me! On our two-year anniversary!

We talked about marriage lately. Or sort of. He mentioned wanting to settle down, thinking it was time for things to change. He had actually said that last week—"Amy, I think I'm ready for a change. Ready to settle down." And he gave me that look. You know the one—the look that says *I'm saying something between the lines here.*

I get goosebumps just thinking about it.

I realize it's nine o'clock, and I've been sitting in my car for a half hour. Not that it matters. I pay for this space annually. I can sit here all year if I want to. But I don't.

I drive slowly home, my meager box of belongings sitting beside me in the passenger seat of my little Escort, the traffic ticket sticking out of the top. I carry the box up to my apartment and shower.

I might as well look nice for tonight. Since I have nothing better to do (like be at work), I make an appointment to get my nails done at 11:00 and one to get my hair done at 4:00. After my manicure, I have a light lunch at a cute café near the University and do a little shopping to keep my mind occupied. I pick up a pocket watch for Bart. It's a bit pricey, but after all, we *are* celebrating two years. And maybe more. The sales clerk asks if I want it engraved and I decide that I do.

Bart...loving you for two years...looking forward to a lifetime! Love, Amy It's a lot to fit on a watch, but the clerk makes it work.

Bart calls at three o'clock to say he's in town and going to take a short nap. We talk for about two minutes. He sounds really tired.

The day seems to drag on forever.

Finally, 4:00 comes, and it's time for my hair appointment. I have her put it in a soft updo with a few little ringlets around my face.

"Don't ever color your hair," my stylist says, something she repeats every time I come in. I have light brown hair with natural highlights. I really do like my natural color. "This style really shows off those gorgeous blue eyes of yours."

She doesn't finish until nearly six, so I have just enough time to put on my dress and pick out some jewelry. I choose the small dangling opals Bart got for me last Christmas. He said the soft colors and the way they reflected light reminded him of my eyes.

I look at myself in my full-length mirror, and I'm happy with the result. The dress is a soft blue, almost turquoise, and shows just enough cleavage to be interesting, but not slutty.

I feel beautiful both inside and outside. Bart wants me. *Me*. My job loss doesn't seem so awful now.

I glance at my watch. 6:45 p.m. Fifteen minutes until the night I'll always remember begins.

I grab my cell phone and punch in Mom's number. "Mom?"

"Hello, dear," Mom says. "I'm baking peach cobbler. You know how your dad loves it."

"I thought you said he had high cholesterol."

"He does. But that walk wore us out. We need a pick-me-up."

"Oh," I say. "Mom, I've got to talk fast because Bart is on his way over to get me, but guess what?"

"What?" I can tell Mom is licking a spoon.

"I think he's going to propose!"

"What?" The kitchen background noise stops. "Really? Oh, honey, that is *so* exciting. How do you know?"

"It's our two-year anniversary. He told me he's taking me someplace really special and I should dress up."

"That is *so* exciting!" Mom says again. "Call me afterwards."

"If it's not too late." I hear the buzzer to my apartment door. "Gotta go. Love you."

I let Bart in. He's dressed in a light blue button down and dark blue cotton pants with a navy sport coat. I can't help but notice we match.

"Hi, honey." I kiss him. He pulls me into him for a longer kiss.

"You missed me?" I say.

"I just want to remember what you feel like tonight," he says.

Oh, he wants to remember this night forever too!! My stomach does a flip-flop.

We go downstairs and climb into his BMW.

"Where are we going?" I ask.

"You'll see."

He takes me into downtown Ann Arbor, and we park in the structure at the corner of William and Fourth. I try to figure out what's around here. Palio. The Real Seafood Company. Gratzi. And...

"Oh my gosh!" I say, realizing where he must be taking me. Bart gives me a little smile but says nothing. We walk a few blocks. It's chilly out and but there's no snow. In March in Michigan, you never know which way the weather will go. I pull my wrap around me and stick my hand down inside Bart's jacket pocket to warm it. I feel a small box about the size of a ring box. Bart quickly takes my hand out and holds it, giving it a little squeeze. I have butterflies in my stomach but say nothing. After all, he wants this to be a surprise.

We turn a corner and then there it is, in front of us. The Emerald Forest.

"Bart...really?"

"Amy, you've been wanting to come here forever. I kept promising you and...well, here we are."

The Emerald Forest is Ann Arbor's most romantic restaurant. It's also very hard to get into; you have to make reservations at least two weeks in advance.

It's a popular place for couples and special occasions, not so much because it's an expensive four-star restaurant—which it is—but because of the atmosphere.

You literally feel like you're in a forest at night, minus the mosquitoes. Around the perimeter of the room, hiding the walls, are vines and fake (but really realistic) trees. They're also scattered out in the open room, giving each table some privacy. Some tables are near a pond. Ours is in a glen of flowers near a small waterfall. All of the trees have small white lights in them, and several trees have soft lanterns hanging from them. There is a candle on each table.

There are also stars above us and a crescent moon. It sounds gaudy and fake, but it's not. It's very well done and elegant. You feel like you're at a private garden party.

The waiter brings out menus, pours water, and takes our drink orders. After the waiter leaves, Bart excuses himself to use the restroom. He leaves his jacket on the back of his chair.

11

The room is dimly lit. I could easily slide the ring out of his pocket and take a quick look before he gets back. He'll never know.

But don't I want to be surprised? This is, after all, a big night for me. Do I really want a sneak peek?

I glance toward the restrooms. Here comes Bart. Too late.

We order our food, and Bart's phone rings.

"Amy, I have to take this," he says.

"Oh, Bart…"

"Last call. I promise. Then I'll turn it off."

He gets up, walks back toward the restrooms, and disappears.

Oh, what the heck. I slip my hand into his pocket and pull out the box.

It's light blue—from Tiffany's. I catch my breath. Then I open it.

Inside is the most exquisite, most incredible diamond I have ever seen, set in a silver band with tiny diamond chips all around. An engagement ring. Wow. He must have paid a fortune. Did I mention that he was rich?

I snap it shut and stick it back in his pocket. I can't wait to try it on. I can't believe I'm going to be Mrs. Bart Carlton.

When will he give it to me? Before we eat? Then we could talk about our plans. Or later, after dessert? Or will he slip it to the waiter to put *in* the dessert?

"Amy, you look happy tonight," Bart says, slipping into his seat. "Did you have a good day at work?"

"Ah…yes. Well…no…" I don't want to bring up my job loss or my car accident right now. Not tonight. "I'm just so happy to be here," I say, sweeping my eyes around the room and then back to meet his. "With you."

I expect Bart to gaze longingly back into my eyes, but instead he leans back in his chair. "Amy, we've been together a long time…" There's a strange tone to his voice. Maybe he's nervous.

"Yes," I say. "Two years. Two years today, actually."

"Well…" he sighs. "Look, I'm not sure how to do this, but I want to do it right. You're a nice girl. You deserve at least this much."

I'm a bit confused. I'm a *nice girl?*
"What I'm trying to say is…"
"Yes?"
"I want to break up with you."
There's a long silence at the table. The waiter brings our bread and refills our water glasses.
"What?"
"I want to break up with you. Amy, we had some fun. We had some good times, but you don't really fit into my life."
"But…" I swallow. "We're so close. We share so much, and I know you so well."
"Not really," Bart says. "I haven't been entirely truthful with you."
"What do you mean?"
"Last year, when I made partner? Well, I told you I was going off to do some pro-bono work in Haiti to give the firm a good rep."
"Yes." My stomach sinks just a little.
"I was really at their Birmingham office. I work a lot of hours there. I have a cot right in my office. Or rather, a pull-out couch."
I really can't wrap my mind around what he's saying. This is not the way this night was supposed to go. I had my hair done. I twist my fingers around one of my ringlet curls, wondering how I had been so wrong.
"But we have so much fun together," I say. "I mean… we…" At the moment, I can't quite think of what we do besides eat out and go to the occasional movie. Bart is always so busy with work.
We had talked about our future. About how he wanted a big house in the city with a cottage up north. And a boat. We were going to go boating.
"We wanted a boat," I say. This cannot be happening. He's supposed to ask me to marry him.
"I thought you loved me," I say. "I thought we had plans. I thought you wanted to spend the rest of your life with me."
I'm getting angry now. I feel the heat rise in my face.
"Amy…"

"What about the ring?" I say, suddenly pointing across the table, startling him.

"The ring?" he says.

"The ring in your pocket. There's an engagement ring from Tiffany's in your jacket pocket."

"What have you been doing, rifling through my pockets?" Now he's angry.

"I felt it when I stuck my hand down in your pocket on the street."

"It's not a ring," he says.

"It is. I peeked. You were going to ask me to marry you, and at some point, you changed your mind. I got my hair done. My nails done. I'm wearing the dress you love." Part of my mind tells me I sound ridiculous, but I can't stop myself. "I love you! You were supposed to ask me to marry you tonight on our two-year anniversary!"

"Amy…the ring is for someone else."

"Someone else? You're buying rings for other people now?"

"It's someone in the firm, at the Birmingham office. My secretary."

Of course.

"I've been seeing her for a year now."

"What?" How could I have not known?

"At first, it was just a fling. You're a nice girl, and I thought if it didn't work out between her and me…but she's so fun, Amy. We go rollerblading together and shopping for antiques. Last fall we went snorkeling in the Bahamas. I'm sorry, Amy, you're just not that fun . You're just so…writerly."

Tears sting my eyes. I blink them away. I will *not* cry in front of him.

"She's pregnant. I'm going to ask her to marry me. Probably later tonight. But I thought I'd take care of this first."

"But you brought me *here*." I gesture around the room, at the restaurant I'd always dreamed of coming to.

"I owed you this. I promised I'd bring you here someday, and I don't want to be known as a man who breaks his promises."

He stands up.
"Goodbye, Amy. Have a nice life."
And he picks up his jacket and walks out of the restaurant.

Chapter Two

I don't sleep all night. After giving the waiter Bart's contact information so he can bill him for the food we didn't eat, I take a taxi home, undress, and go to bed to cry into my pillow. Finally, at 7 a.m., Mouser starts rubbing against my face so I get up.

It's then I remember I don't have a job to go to.

I glance at the book on my nightstand. *Positive self-talk*, I remind myself.

I wander into the kitchen in my pajamas and feed the cat. I see my heels by the door where I took them off last night. And my dress crumpled on the floor.

"Idiot!" My anger flares again. I'm not sure whom I'm calling an idiot, myself or Bart. How could I have been so dumb?

Tears form in my eyes again, and I grab my phone and start downloading break-up songs. My first choice is "I Will Always Love You" by Whitney Houston. Then comes "Nothing Compares to You" by Sinead O'Connor. I start sobbing.

A text comes in. I look at my phone.

Well? It's from Mom.

I ignore it.

Mom again. **Text me a photo of the ring when you get up.**

I wipe the tears from my eyes and don't answer. What am I going to tell my mom?

Another text comes in. This one is from Andrea.

You left yr calendar here. Want me 2 save it for u?

At that point, I get angrier. My job and my boyfriend in the same day? The next song I download is "I Will Survive" by Gloria Gaynor. Then I search and come up with an angry music playlist for a woman scorned. I put my earbuds in and start cleaning the apartment. I clean when I'm upset. I always have. It keeps my mind busy and gives my hands something to do. It makes me feel better.

I am above this. I can carry on. I can become a new me in 30 days or less.

Positive self-talk.

Fueled by Beyoncé's "Irreplaceable," I scrub out the shower. I clean out the fridge to Carrie Underwood's "Before He Cheats." I clean, varnish, and polish to the tune of every angry chick song I can find.

When I finish, it's early afternoon.

I look at my box of stuff from the office.

Boring?

Not fun?

I go to my closet. Lined up neatly are the skirts and blouses that I've worn to work for the past five years. In one sweep of my arms, I grab them and stuff them into a bag. Then my shoes. Practical shoes. My black flats, my black pumps. Heck, I'll get rid of the other colors too.

I pick the turquoise dress up off the floor and add it to the bag.

Still listening to music, I comb the apartment for every photo I can find of Bart. I cut them into tiny pieces and throw those into the shredder. With a flourish, I turn it on.

With a big bag full of most of my clothes and the bag of shredded photos, I trek out into the apartment's garage and stuff them into the trunk of my car.

Mrs. Crabbs is in the hall getting her paper when I come back upstairs.

"Still in your pajamas?" she asks, scornfully looking me up and down.

I let myself back into my apartment and pull on some jeans and a fresh T-shirt.

Then I go back down to my car.

Mom and Andrea both text again. Mom wants me to call her.

Where R U? Andrea texts. **Calendar? Also, wanted to take you out. So sorry. Miss u here!**

I ignore them and drive to the mall, where I know there are recycle bins and a clothing bin for the needy in the parking lot.

17

I throw the bag of shredded photos into a recycle bin and the clothes into the bin that looks like a large mailbox. As my clothes slide down and the flap closes shut, I rub my hands together.

"Goodbye old me," I say.

I'm feeling better already. Just as Myra Winnrey says in her book, I'll reinvent myself. The new me will be a better me, a more exciting me. I don't need a boyfriend. I don't need a job. Maybe I'll write a novel. I'll buy some Bohemian clothes and wear beads and live off beans and rice while I write. I make a mental note to search for pictures of Bohemian clothes on the Internet when I get home.

On my way home, I notice I'm nearly out of gas so I pull into the gas station.

As I'm pumping, some gas spills on my hands. I reach into the back seat and pull out a new canister of hand wipes. I open it and try to pull some through the slot on the top. They won't come. My hands smell, so I try again. There's a warning across the top that says, "Don't poke finger into slot." But maybe...I stick my finger in just a smidgeon and grab the tip of the first cloth to pull it through. When I pull back, my finger gets stuck in the lid opening and the little prongs dig in.

It hurts. A lot. I shake my hand, trying to lose the thing, because pulling it out isn't going to be an option. The lid pops off the canister but is firmly embedded in my finger.

"Hi, Amy," says an all-too-familiar voice. I look up. It's Bart. My hair's a mess, my jeans are ripped, and last night's makeup is smeared with dried tears. Not the way you want your ex to find you.

He smiles and glances at the canister lid. "Looks like you finally got a ring on your finger," he says, and gives a little laugh. "Hang tight, Amy. You're a nice girl."

Before I can answer, he walks back to the gas station and goes inside. Grumbling under my breath with all sorts of nasty words and fighting back more tears, I pull the thing off my finger, cutting myself in the process. Then I get in the car and close the door. I see Bart walking out of the gas station. He's with a blond woman, and her side is toward me so I can't get a good look at her face. From the outline of her side view, though, I can see she is definitely very pregnant. She has her hand stuck in the back pocket of his pants. When he opens the car door for her, she pulls it out and some papers come out with it. Her hand glints in the light. The ring.

He shuts the door and gets in, turning long enough to give me a little salute. Then they drive away.

I sniff and rifle through my purse for some change because I need a bottle of water. As I walk toward the gas station, I glance at the papers that dropped from Bart's pocket. I stop and bend down to pick them up.

One is a gas station receipt. The other is a lottery ticket.

I stuff them both into my purse and go inside. I buy my water and two cans of tuna and drive home.

On my way to my apartment, I grab the mail and stop at Mrs. Burgess's door, the elderly lady I help out on occasion. When she opens it, I hand her the mail.

"Thank you, Amy," she says. Mrs. Burgess is the sweetest woman I know. Her husband passed away a few years ago, and she doesn't have any other family. We've become good friends.

"I got that tuna you asked for the other day," I say. Mrs. Burgess's cat only eats tuna, not cat food.

"Thank you, dear. Would you like to come in for a cup of tea? You look like you're upset. Have you been crying?"

"No, I'm fine," I say, rubbing my hand over my face. I can tell she doesn't believe me, but Mrs. Burgess is an easy friend. She lets me go.

Inside my apartment, I run my finger under some water to clean it up and then find a bandage. Bart's cruel words ring through my head, and I can't get the picture of that woman—his *other* woman—out of my head.

"You'll be alright, Amy. Who needs him anyway?" I say, practicing my positive self-talk.

There's a bottle of wine on the counter. I don't usually drink, so I don't normally have alcohol around. But this is a bottle I got at my brother's wedding. It's one of those fancy ones where the label has the couple's name on it and "Happily Ever After" in script across the front. Mom told me to keep it forever as a souvenir.

I uncork it and take a swig. I figure I should have something to eat with it, so I grab the tub of chocolate chip cookie dough ice cream out of the freezer and sit down on the couch with a spoon and my bottle of wine.

The next song on my playlist is "Need You Now" by Lady Antebellum, not exactly a power woman song. I listen to it and start to cry again.

Eventually, I get tired of music and turn on the TV. There's a science program about geese and how they mate for life. It seems everybody is in love except me.

I channel hop, watching various shows. Then I see that the Hallmark Channel is playing *You've Got Mail*, a favorite older movie of mine. A chick flick.

Somewhere near the end, just before the happily ever after, I fall asleep.

When I wake up, my head is throbbing and light is streaming across the room.

"Meow?" Mouser is rubbing against my hand, which is hanging limply over the side of the couch.

I turn and see the bottle of wine, lying empty on the floor. The ice cream carton is also empty. I vaguely remember throwing up somewhere in the middle of the night.

I moan and sit up. My head protests. This is why I never get drunk. Why do people party only to feel this way the next morning?

I stagger into the kitchen, take some aspirin, and drink some water. Then I search the Internet (purposefully not using InterFind's search engine) to find a cure for a hangover. They all sound disgusting, so I eat a plain piece of toast and try to rehydrate myself with more water.

Then I sit on the couch to take stock of my situation.

I'm jobless and can only survive about three months on my savings and severance. I'm single. *Really* single. And as far as I can see, I don't have many clothes left.

There's a knock on my door.

"Amy?" I hear my mom's voice, and it sounds shrill and worried.

I freeze. I'm not ready to talk to anybody yet. And I think I'm still a bit drunk.

"Herb, you need to break down her door," I hear Mom say.
"Gladys, there's no need to do that. I'm sure the manager has a key."
I race over and open the door, the movement making my head pound.
"Amy!" Mom says and throws herself at me, giving me a huge hug. Dad is just staring. I know I look awful. I haven't showered.
"You smell like alcohol," Mom says, pulling away. Then she frowns. "Amy, we've been worried sick about you. I've texted and called about a hundred times. You haven't answered. You were supposed to call me after Bart proposed."
Then she stops short and looks down at my finger. My empty ring finger.
"Oh, honey," Mom says, and hugs me again, this time more tenderly. Dad comes over and pats my shoulder.
"Do I need to go after that fella with my baseball bat?" Dad says. That's what he has said to me since I was little, always threatening with a baseball bat any boy who hurt me. Of course, in reality, Dad would never hurt a fly.
They come in and close the door, and I tell them the whole story. I share that Bart hasn't asked me yet and actually broke up with me, which is why I didn't call her. I was too upset. I leave out the part about the pregnant girlfriend because that part is just too humiliating.
It's then that I look at my phone and see 27 unread texts and five missed phone calls from my mom.
"I'm sorry," I say and hiccup.
Mom spots the empty wine bottle on the floor just as Dad picks up the empty carton of ice cream and throws it away.
"You drank Tad and Darlene's bottle of wine?" Mom is incredulous. "It was a *keepsake.*"
"Well, I still have the bottle," I say.
Mom picks up the bottle and turns it over as if it's made of gold. "It was from their *wedding,*" she says softly.
"It's no big deal," says my dad.
My parents are pretty cool. They don't usually badger me about things, and I can tell it's painful for her, but Mom lets it go. I give Dad a knowing "thank you" smile.

21

I slump back down on the couch. "I'm not really up for visiting," I say. "I'll be okay. I realized I don't need Bart. I just need some time to think."

Mom looks uncertain.

"Gladys, let's leave her alone now that we know she's okay," Dad says.

"I don't know..." Mom says, but Dad puts his arm around her shoulders.

"Come on, Gladys," he says.

"Call us if you need anything," Mom says. "I mean *anything*, Amy, okay?" Then, reluctantly, Mom hugs me and they leave.

Next, I text Andrea and tell her to throw the calendar away and that I'll call her in a day or so to get together.

Then I grab a bowl of cereal and turn the TV back on.

I flip through some channels. I might as well waste away as a couch potato. I am, after all, boring and nice. Isn't that what boring people do? I pause at *Ellen* and watch her opening remarks and little dance, then move on to a game show. After that, is the 12:00 news.

There was a fire downtown in an apartment complex. The new school board is squabbling about salaries.

The perky newscaster is smiling through it all. "And next, we'll give you last night's lottery numbers in case you missed them."

Something stirs inside my brain. Lottery numbers.

Just then, my phone rings. It's Andrea. I sigh and answer.

"Hey," she says, quietly. "I found you a job. It's perfect. My cousin is hiring down at the Towne Post and she said if you can come for an interview now—like within the next hour—you can probably have the job. A *writing* job."

"What? Really?" I turn off the TV. "Why are you whispering?"

"I'm at my desk. Should I tell her you're coming?"

"Uh...yeah. Yes! I'll be there in an hour."

"Just talk to the receptionist in the lobby and ask for Anna. Tell her who you are. Dress business-like—they're kind of conservative over there."

I hang up. God bless Andrea! She is always thinking of me.

I run into the bathroom and quickly wash up and put makeup on. Then I go to my closet and realize I don't have a thing to wear. Literally.

I start to panic. I had perfect skirts, blouses, and shoes, and I threw them all away. What was I thinking? I glance at my phone. I don't have time to go clothes shopping. I only have $20 on hand, anyway. I cut up my credit card last month for chapter six in my *Claiming Happiness* book. Having zero debt is supposed to free you.

I have no choice. I'll have to get my clothes back.

I drive back to the mall where I donated them and think for a moment about running in and grabbing something off the rack. And paying with what? My looks? I could open up a new credit card with the department store.

But I have a whole wardrobe in that box in front of me. A *whole wardrobe*. So I get out of my car and try to peek in the donation box. The sign says that pick-up is at the end of the month, so my clothes are all still in there. If I can just reach my arm inside it, maybe I can grab my bag. I try. There isn't quite enough room but if I could get up higher and maybe reach down inside I could get it.

I spot a shopping cart nearby, so I roll it up to the donation mailbox and carefully step inside of it. It wiggles a little but doesn't roll. I open the donation box again and reach my arm down inside. I can feel plastic. Yes! It's my plastic bag! My clothes! I give a tug but the bag is too big to fit back up through the mail slot.

Maybe I can tear open the bag and take out one article of clothing at a time. I fiddle with the twist tie I put on it and feel some fabric. I pull. Out comes my black skirt. *Yes!*

Now to get a blouse to match. The first article of clothing I grab is a scarf. That won't work. I reach back down in and the shopping cart wobbles. A few passersby are looking at me. I smile at them and dig in again. There's something silky – maybe a blouse. If I can just get an outfit out now, I can call the company and ask them to let me in to get the rest out later.

Then I hear a couple of blips of a police siren. I look up.

"Ma'am, please step back," says a police officer, getting out of his car.

"What? I…"

The shopping cart wiggles again.

"Ma'am, step back from the donation mailbox."

I can't believe this. Not now!

"No, you don't understand. These are my clothes. I put them in here by mistake. I just need to get this blouse out and some shoes." I turn toward the officer and the shopping cart moves. I lose my balance, it rolls out from under me, and I fall forward, pitching off the cart. The officer is quick and grabs me before I hit the blacktop. I'm clutching the blouse in my hands.

He sets me down on my feet.

"Are you okay?" he asks.

"Um. Well…"

"Ma'am, I have to place you under arrest for attempted theft."

"But these are my clothes!" I say.

"You were looting from private property. Those belong to the Sisters of Need."

"No, they're *my* clothes. I didn't mean to put them in here."

But he's steering me toward the car. "I'll also have to ask you to take a breathalyzer test," he says.

"What? No! I don't even drink. Well, except last night, but that's different and it's not my fault. It's my ex-boyfriend's."

He's pushing my head down and putting me inside the car. I can't believe this. I'm being arrested.

Apparently, I'm sober, which is a relief, but I have to call my parents to bail me out. The Sisters of Need aren't going to press charges if I agree to leave my clothes in the donation bin so that women in need of jobs can use them for interview clothes. Which is what I need as well, but I don't mention that.

Mom chalks it all up to grief over my breakup, and she and Dad take me back to their house and make me some comfort food for dinner. I text Andrea to tell her I had an emergency and missed the interview but thank you anyway. Then I get in my car (which Dad had driven back to his house from the mall) to head back to my apartment with a bag of leftover food. Mom is worried, I can tell. I had to explain everything to them about the clothes and the job.

On the way home, I pass a thrift store. Since I only have the one pair of jeans (which I'm wearing), I decide to go in and get myself some clothes. I can't afford to shop retail now—I'm jobless.

With a heavy sigh, I go in. It's not even one of those nice second-hand stores. It's a thrift shop. The clothes are organized by size, and most smell of mothballs.

I finger a shirt half-heartedly and then walk over to the jeans. Is this what my life has come to? I stare at the rack of jeans and just can't make myself try them on. Not because they're used. More because I'm tired and my arm hurts from reaching into the bin and I have black ink on my fingers from my fingerprinting at the police station. I feel tears sting my eyes.

"Can I help you?" someone asks. I turn, and there's a woman standing there with a stack of clothes and some hangers. She's wearing a name badge that shows she works here.

"Um…" I blink back the tears. On top of the woman's stack is a silky purple scarf with some shiny silver threads running through it. "Actually, that's just what I was looking for." I reach over and take the scarf from her.

"That color will look good on you," she says.

I take it to the counter to pay so I can go home.

"That'll be two dollars," says the tired-looking woman behind the cash register.

I open my purse and see the small gift in there. Bart's watch. I dig past it for my wallet. I pull out my twenty-dollar bill, and that's when I see the lottery ticket. I had forgotten all about it. The lottery ticket Bart dropped.

Actually, I think, *his pregnant girlfriend* with her *hand* in his trouser pocket dropped it. The hand that was wearing the ring from Tiffany's.

I feel tears sting my eyes again, and I quickly head out to my car. It's dark outside by now. I sit there for a moment, wiping my eyes, and thinking. What if? What if the ticket is a winner? I dig it out again and see that it's for the Mega Millions. I try to look the numbers up on my phone but I can't get good coverage and the Thrift Store obviously doesn't have Wi-Fi. Frustrated, I drive home.

Mrs. Burgess is standing out in the hall when I dash up to my apartment. Her arms are wrapped around her. "Are you okay?" I ask.

"A pipe broke," she says. "My living room is a mess."

The landlord and some people are in there, sucking up the water with a noisy machine. They're just finishing.

"That's as good as it's going to get, ma'am," one of them says. "Just stay out of the living room tonight."

The plumber leaves, saying everything is okay.

"Let's go in and move your TV into the kitchen and see what I can do to help you," I say. I stay with her about an hour, moving furniture and getting her things that she needs—her reading glasses, her knitting. The workers left everything piled in a corner.

Grateful, she sits down in her chair as I leave, and her cat jumps in her lap.

"Are you going to be okay now?" I ask.

"You're such a dear," she says. "Thank you, Amy."

By the time I get home, it's so late and I'm so depressed from my day that I climb out of my only pair of jeans and go to bed without dinner. The package of leftovers Mom sent home is spoiled now anyway.

Chapter Three

The next morning I wake with a start, thinking I'm late for work. Then it all comes crashing back down on me.

Without washing up, I wander into the kitchen, feed the cat, and grab some cereal and milk. Then I plop myself down in front of the television for another day of couch potato life.

It's the morning news. There was a fire in a downtown department store last night. Nobody was hurt, but a large number of Vera Wang handbags burned to a crisp. There's construction on Maple and Miller Roads, so drivers are expected to bypass that area. Of course, this doesn't apply to those of us who don't have a job to drive to.

I take another bite of cereal.

My phone beeps with a text. I look at it. Andrea again.

Lunch?

I text back. **No.**

I'll drop your calendar off on my lunch hour.

I sigh but type in **ok**. I really don't want to see anybody right now.

I'm still sitting on the couch when Andrea arrives. I've worked my way through the morning news, a talk show, and a game show. It's time for the 12 o'clock news.

It's blaring in the background when I open the door and let Andrea in. She hands me my calendar, and then her eyes travel up and down me. I'm unwashed and wearing my pajamas.

"Amy." She sits herself down in the chair next to my sofa. She grabs the remote and clicks off the television. "Oh, Amy." She shakes her head. "All of this over a job?"

"No. Not just a job." I sniff. Then tears come to my eyes.

"Amy?" Andrea is worried.

She's my best friend so I find myself telling her about Bart (except for the pregnant girlfriend) and then crying all over again. I'm a mess.

"You're a mess," Andrea says, as if reading my mind. "Honey, you need to get out of the house. Go for a walk. Go for a coffee."

I sniff. She's right. This is no way to act. Bart and his pregnant fiancée are probably looking at maternity wedding gowns and buying baby cribs right now.

"You're right," I say.

Andrea looks at her phone. "I need to get back to the office. Lunch hour is almost over." We give each other a hug. At the door, she turns and points to me. "Get out of the apartment for a few hours. I'm going to check in later to see what you did."

After she's gone, I sit back down on the couch and turn the TV on. A commercial comes on for Myra Winnrey's show, my favorite, which is on later this afternoon. One of the segments is about living your dream. After the commercial is over, I turn the television off with the remote and sit there.

What is *my* dream? Do I even have one?

I've always wanted to write. Always. And I was doing that.

Depressed, I turn the TV on again. There's a news brief.

"And the winner of the Mega Millions lottery still hasn't come forward to claim their prize," says the announcer. "More tonight at 5 p.m."

My stomach jumps.

The lottery ticket!

What if…?

I stifle my excitement and dig through my purse, pushing aside the wrapped pocket watch. I find the ticket, grab my phone, and Google the lottery numbers. I find a video clip replaying the drawing.

"Here are the numbers for the $22 million jackpot," says the perky lottery girl. The numbers pop up on the screen, and the perky girl reads them.

5…

I have one of those.

12…

And that number.

15…34… 46…

Oh my gosh. My stomach does a flip-flop as I follow the numbers.

52.

I stare at my ticket. I look back at the phone screen and squint to be sure. Quickly, I take a screen shot of the lottery numbers.

I go over them again. Then again.

It's a winning ticket. It's worth $22 million.

A small sound escapes my lips. I'm not sure if it's a squeal or a whimper. That jerk, that awful jerk, has just won $22 million. Where is the justice in this life? Where?

But wait.

I have the ticket. And he doesn't know it.

Oh my gosh.

Oh my gosh!

What do I do? Do I tell him? Do I keep it? *Does* he know?

I glance at the ticket again to see if it's an easy pick or if he chose the numbers. There's no way of knowing.

Hmmmm.

It doesn't seem right to keep it. It is, after all, his ticket.

But I'm jobless and jilted. And he lied to me. *Lied* to me.

Another vision of the pregnant, blond girlfriend flashes through my mind.

I call Andrea.

"Hello?"

"Andrea. It's Amy."

"You sound perkier than you did a while ago," Andrea says.

"Listen. I have a question. If you found something that you knew belonged to somebody else but that somebody else wasn't deserving of it, would you keep it or return it?"

"Last winter, I saw a man drop a cashmere scarf on the street, and I picked it up to give to him. Then I saw him kick the dog he was walking. I kept the scarf and sold it on eBay. Made $35."

"Okay. Thanks."

I hang up and call Mom.

"Mom, if I keep something that technically isn't mine, is it wrong?"

"Of course, it's wrong dear. Did you find somebody's cell phone? Because Dad found somebody's cell phone that they left in the bathroom at this restaurant and he turned it in."

"Mom. It's not a cell phone. It's…it's a cashmere scarf."

"Did you see who dropped it?"

"Um…not really."

"I'd try to sell it on eBay. You don't want to wear it. It might have lice."

I hang up.

I'm not sure that was helpful. I sit there, holding the ticket, thinking. What am I going to do? Call Bart and say, "Honey, I'm so sorry we broke up but I found your lottery ticket. It's worth $22 million, and I thought you'd want it back. Maybe you could use the money to buy your pregnant girlfriend a nice house and buy some toys for the baby."

I decide to get some fresh air. Carefully, I tuck the ticket inside the wallet pocket of my purse and then change my mind and slip it behind a framed photo of Mouser on my wall, in between the photo and the matting. Then I brush my teeth and hair and go downstairs to get the mail. It's sunny outside and kind of warm for March.

I take the mail back upstairs and knock on Mrs. Burgess's door.

"Here you go," I say when she opens the door. I notice my hands are shaking as I hand her the mail. She's wearing her robe, and her hair is in curlers. That's unusual because she's always dressed for the day and even wears lipstick, though she hardly goes out.

"Oh, Amy," she says. "My husband's pension checks have stopped because with the plan he had I only get them so long after his death. But I'm behind on rent, and if I don't pay soon, they're going to kick me out."

"What?"

Mrs. Burgess has lived here as long as I can remember. Longer than I have, and I have been here nearly four years.

"He had all these medical bills from when he was sick, you know, and…"

She looks distraught. All of this on top of what happened with her water pipe? Her cat, Fluff, comes by and rubs against her legs.

"Where will we go?" But then she straightens her back and gives me her usual Mrs. Burgess smile. "Oh, honey, it'll be all right. Listen to me bantering on. The good Lord has taken care of me this long. I don't expect He'll let me down now."

My mind is twirling. If I cash that lottery ticket, I can help her.

"How much do you need?" I ask.

"Why don't you come in for tea?"

I do. The living room carpet is dry, and I help her move her furniture back in place, despite her demands that I rest. She puts on a pot for tea.

Mrs. Burgess's apartment is cluttered but clean. All of the surfaces are covered with little mementos and photos from the days when she and her husband traveled, before he got sick. The walls are lined with bookshelves, and postcards are stuck in the corners of picture frames. Doilies are draped here and there. Most every square inch is covered with something.

But I love it here. I have spent many afternoons here, sipping tea and discussing the stresses of work or just about anything life brought my way. Mrs. Burgess always has a way of making it feel better.

But today I need to make her feel better.

Only it doesn't happen that way.

"Why aren't you at work, Amy?" she says. "And you don't look so well."

So I begin to tell her about Bart, the supposed engagement dinner, and how it ended. I even throw in the part about the pregnant girlfriend and all the months of cheating. But I don't mention the lottery ticket.

"How could I be so stupid?" I say. I'm crying now.

Mrs. Burgess says the usual things, about how it will be okay, about how I'm not boring and quite nearly the best friend she has at the moment. Then I start wondering what I'll do if she does move out and I don't have her across the hall from me anymore.

I cry harder.

"I don't want you to leave," I say.

She hands me more tissues. "I don't want to leave either, Amy. This is my home. But some things can't be helped. We can still visit each other."

Or I can cash the ticket and help her out.

I sit in my apartment looking at the framed photo. I can't cash it today. If Bart knew those numbers, he (after a frantic search of his pants, his past paths, and his apartment) will be standing outside of the state lottery department, waiting. If he sees me, he'll put two and two together and he'll know. He'll use his lawyer powers to take it from me, and then I won't be able to help Mrs. Burgess.

Or maybe I can't cash it at all. Will I go to jail? Is it legally his?

I do a web search on what happens if you find a winning lottery ticket. What I learn is that most stores have video cameras so they will be able to see the time and place that a ticket was purchased.

In Arkansas, there was a case just last year where a woman tried to cash a "found" lottery ticket, but the original owner claimed it and she had to turn over the money because the store had the date and time stamp on the video of the original man buying it.

Then I do a search on security videos and find that most stores record over them within a few weeks.

If I wait long enough, there won't be any proof.

I sigh and lean back on the couch. I'm a goody-goody. All part of my being boring, I guess. So there's no way I'll risk cashing it. No way.

But that doesn't mean I have to give it to him.

I glance at the framed picture of Mouser again. Why did Bart have to do this to me? I hate men. All men.

I put my earbuds in again and think about the words of my former boss. *I'm boring.*

He's a man too.

I can't help but start to cry again, and it makes me feel pathetic. Pathetic is no good. Make a decision, Amy.

I decide to wait a while and then cash it.

I have three months of savings. I call our landlady and explain that I have just lost a job but am getting a new one. (Not really a lie...just sort of.) If she can just wait several weeks, I can pay both my rent and Mrs. Burgess's rent (anonymously) in full and will give her interest. After a lengthy talk, she agrees. We're good tenants, and she doesn't want to lose either of us.

Then I lay low for a few weeks. I do the normal things – go to lunch with Andrea, visit my parents, clean the apartment and try to act normal. I let Mom take me shopping for a few clothes and half-heartedly look for a job in case something happens and I don't get the lottery money.

Mostly, though, I sit on the couch and watch TV or read magazines. Despite the fact that I could be really rich in a few weeks, I remember the words of my boss and my ex. I'm boring.

So will that change when I'm rich?

All I have ever wanted to do is write. My degree is in journalism and marketing, but there was a shortage of jobs due to most papers going digital and writers around the country submitting stories for free. I liked my job at InterFind writing ad copy, but now that's gone. And I don't really want to leave Ann Arbor. I graduated from the university here, and I love this town. Plus, my parents live close by.

So what will I do with my life?

I sigh and turn off the TV. I'll wait to get the money and then I'll see.

After about six weeks, I tie the purple scarf around my head, put some sunglasses on, and go to the Lottery headquarters in Lansing. When the clerk asks if she can help me, I carefully pull the ticket out of my pocket.

"I've won," I say. "And I want to remain anonymous."

It's in my bank account! All of that money! Minus the taxes, of course. I've been discreet, and so far nobody, not even my parents, realize. It's so hard to keep a secret this big, but I haven't yet figured out a way to spend any of it without alerting Bart.

But my mind is working overtime on a plan.

I am so giddy with excitement and nerves I can hardly sleep. Oh my gosh. What a girl can do with money! After I pay our rent (anonymously), the first thing I do is go shopping and replace some of the clothes I threw out. I don't get anything fancy for fear of alerting people I'm suddenly rich. But I get several pairs of comfy jeans and some nice tops, and I splurge on a Vera Bradley handbag.

Then I take Andrea out to lunch.

"How's the job hunt going?" she asks, eyeing my bag. "Nice bag."

Her hair is orange now. Not bright, neon orange, but a more subtle rusty shade. It looks quite nice with her brown eyes.

"So what's your next move?" she asks.

Actually, I'm quite exhausted. It was a lot of work securing the money and figuring out all of the banking stuff and paper signing. And then I've been a nervous wreck since I cashed the ticket, wondering if a police officer was going to show up at my door and arrest me.

But I don't admit that to Andrea. Actually, I have recently asked myself that same question.

"I think I'm going to write a novel," I say. I had been giving it some thought. I can't sit on the couch for the rest of my life and watch TV.

"Really?" She eyes me skeptically. "What kind of novel?"

"Oh, I don't know. Certainly not a romance. Maybe a thriller. Where somebody gets shot."

And that, suddenly, is my new plan.

The next day, I grab my laptop and sit down at my kitchen table. I open it and stare at the blank page. Nothing comes to mind. So I do a search on how to write a novel. Then I search elements of a novel. Character. Storyline. Setting.

Setting. Of course! That's the problem. I need a *place* to write. Some place that will inspire me.

Where do writers go to write? Briefly, images of a sabbatical in Paris flit through my head, but that's not practical. Not without giving away my secret. I need something closer. Cheaper. Where do writers go?

They go to Starbucks.

I grab my laptop, and fueled with new energy to turn my life around, I drive to the nearest Starbucks.

Chapter Four

Three hours later, I'm staring at a blank page. I have nothing. Nothing. I have tried for the murder mystery, but I left my bad-girl heroine dangling on the edge of a cliff, and there was nobody to save her except the cop who had her at gunpoint. And he's a man. There's no way a man is going to save her— this is a girl-power story.

And that's only three pages into it.

I've started over five times. Now I'm contemplating fantasy. You can't go wrong with dragons. Or zombies. Maybe horror?

Oh please God, please God, pleeeease help me to be a better me! I need some direction!

I stand in disgust and go up for another cup of coffee. I will *not* give up.

Or maybe I should. Maybe I could try freelance writing. But who will I query? Or maybe I can write a column for the local paper. It's not like I need to get paid. It could be for free.

Pro bono. Like Bart used to do in Haiti. Or what he had said he was doing...

The line is long. There's a man in front of me with dark, wavy hair. He's wearing soft, worn jeans and a cotton shirt with the sleeves pushed up. He looks very casual, and I can't help noticing he is very handsome. But I'm over men. Forever.

Freelance writing. I turn my mind back to my career. What can I write about? Cats? I can write about the adventures of Mouser. It's not like I do anything else. I'm not even a really good cook so I can't write a cooking column. Until now, I only worked, went out with friends, watched movies, and dated Bart. That has been it.

I could write on how to be a spinster.

Or how to be boring.

I notice people putting their business cards in a fishbowl for a drawing for a free coffee. Out of habit, I reach for mine in my purse and then realize that I don't have one anymore.

Because I don't have a job. I'm nobody. A rich nobody, but a nobody.

Mr. Handsome in front of me is pulling a business card out of his wallet. I wonder what he does? I try to peek over his shoulder but accidently bump him. He turns.

"I'm sorry," I stammer. He has the most incredible blue eyes.

"No worries," he says, turning back. It's his turn now to order. He gets a decaf coffee, black, and drops his card into the fishbowl.

"Decaf?" I say.

He turns those blue eyes back to me.

"You're a caffeine drinker?"

"Yes, definitely. I couldn't get through the day without it!" I giggle. Giggling? Where did that come from?

He looks at me steadily for a moment. "Interesting," he says.

"What do you mean 'interesting?'" I don't like the tone in his voice. I frown at him.

He shrugs. "Most people push themselves too hard. Do too much. So they have to compensate by drinking stimulants."

"What?" I'm getting mad at him and remembering why I hate men. "Why do you think…" I look at his card, lying on top of the others in the fish bowl. "Why do you think, *Josh*, that I am overworked? I can definitely tell you I am *not* overworked. Huh. I've hardly worked at all, as a matter of fact, in the past few weeks."

"Miss?" the clerk says. It's my turn to order. "Coffee. Strong." I say, glancing at Josh. Then I grab some sugar to put in it. I look at his card again. It says *Life Coach*.

"Life Coach?" I say. "What kind of job is a Life Coach, Josh Gray?"

He smiles, not getting the least bit ruffled. Gosh, he's gorgeous.

"I help people make life transitions, like changing jobs. Or I help them figure out what they want out of life, what they want to do, or how they can make a difference by helping them find their strengths."

That stops me. Right here, standing in front of me, is the answer to my prayer. He can help me figure out what I want to do. With my life. With my money. And he's not too hard on the eyes, either.

"Do you want to know more about it? We can discuss it over coffee," he says, raising his cup of decaf. "That is, if you have the time."

"Um…sure." I say, taken aback. After all, it's not like I have a job to get back to.

Back at my table, I close my laptop before he can see what's on it.

"Working?" he asks, nodding at my laptop.

"Yes. I'm writing a novel."

"Oh. Wow. What's it about?"

"It's a murder mystery. Er…fantasy. A murder mystery fantasy. You know, you really can't go wrong with dragons."

Augh! What is wrong with me? He's cute, yes, and perhaps that's distracting me a bit, as are his calm, unwavering blue eyes. But I'm not looking for a cute man. Or a man at all.

He smiles again and shows his perfect white teeth. Not that I notice or anything.

"Pleased to meet you," he says. "And you are?" He holds out his hand.

I shake it. "Amy. Amy Summers."

"So you know what I do. What do you do? Is this your full-time job?"

"Yes. At the moment. Before this…I…uh, worked for InterFind. As a writer."

"Wow. Big company."

"Yeah. It was a big job. A good job."

"What happened?"

"They…downsized." I say.

He shakes his head knowingly. "That has been happening all too often in this economy."

I look across the table at his steady blue eyes. "Actually," I hear myself saying. "They fired me. They let me go because I was 'boring.'" I give a little laugh. I haven't told anyone that before. Not my parents. Not Mrs. Burgess. Not even Andrea knows the truth.

"Boring?"

"And then that same night, my boyfriend dumped me. I thought he was going to propose. He took me out to this plush restaurant and had a ring in his pocket...but it turns out the ring wasn't for me..."

Suddenly, I realize I'm crying. Before I know it, I've told him the entire story of that terrible day—the job loss, the car accident, being dumped. All I leave out is the lottery ticket. Okay, and maybe my arrest and the fact that I threw all my clothes out and got drunk.

"So I'm a mess," I say, using the tissue he hands me to wipe my eyes. "Geez. I'm sorry. You came in here to get a cup of coffee, and you wound up consoling a sobbing, crazy woman."

He laughs. "Not at all. I hear stories like this all the time. Most of my clients have been through something difficult like you have and are at a point where they want to turn their life around and do something completely different."

We're silent for a while. Finally, I ask him, "How did you get into life coaching? That doesn't sound like a job you think of as a kid, like 'I want to be a life coach when I grow up.'"

Josh folds his hands around his coffee cup and stares at it for a moment. "About five years ago, I was working as a construction worker."

I could see that. He has the right muscles for that, certainly.

"My best boyhood friend, Scott, was with me. We got the jobs together. We had big plans, of working, saving money, and then starting our own wood working business someday. Well, one day we were working on this tall building down in Toledo. It was going to be a medical center. We were on the ground attaching large beams to a pulley to be lifted up to the eighth floor. One came loose and fell on Scott. He was standing right next to me when it happened. It could have been me. But it was Scott. It killed him instantly."

"Wow," I say. I can't even imagine someone so close to me dying. The only loved one I've lost was a hamster in fourth grade.

"I couldn't go back to work after the funeral. It just wasn't the same without Scott. And suddenly my dreams were gone. I didn't want to start a company on my own."

I feel tears prick my eyes again.

"So I did some odd jobs for a while, and then one day I met up with a college kid while I was working at a florist. He was on a fast track for med school but was about to drop out of college and join the army. He was there to buy his mom a dozen roses as an 'apology' for his decision. I asked why he felt he should apologize, and he said 'Because it's not what my mom wanted for me.'"

Josh takes a sip of his coffee. His hands are strong. I can suddenly see them holding up large beams or hammering nails into wood.

"I can see that," I say. "The kid not wanting to hurt his mom."

Josh nods.

"So what happened?"

"I asked what he wanted for himself. Turns out he had always dreamed of joining the army but he felt torn about dropping out of medical school, so we figured out a way he could go in the army as an army doctor."

"Wow."

"After that, I knew I liked helping people, so this is what I do now." He's quiet for a moment. "I don't usually tell people that story," he says softly.

Our eyes meet. I wish I knew what it was that I really want to do.

"What about you?" Josh asks, as if reading my mind. "You said that sometimes kids know what they want to become from the time they are little. Are you one of those kids? What did you want to be when you grew up?"

It has been so long since I thought about that. I had plans, big plans, my entire life, but went a safer route after I graduated from high school.

"I wanted to start up a magazine," I say, surprising myself. I had nearly forgotten that dream.

"Really? What's stopping you?"

I think about that. Before, it had always been money. I didn't have the capital to do it. But now...

"Well, I wouldn't really know where to begin," I say.

"I could help you. I'm good at helping people make a plan."

I look into his deep, blue eyes. Maybe, just maybe, I can do it. What if I did? What if I started up my own magazine? I get a trill of excitement in my stomach that I haven't felt in a long time.

"Okay," I say slowly.

"My firm charges a lot..."

"I have the money," I say.

"And we could get grants to help you with the funding for startup costs. I know how to write grants."

"Okay," I say, extending my hand to him. "Let's do it."

Chapter Five

We meet the very next day in my apartment to form a plan. In the back of my mind, I can hear my mom telling me not to invite strange men over to my apartment when I'm alone, but for some reason I feel safe with this guy. I can't imagine Josh putting roofies in my coffee. The worst he'd probably do is swap in a decaf. Josh shows up wearing soft, faded jeans, this time with a pale gray T-shirt that shows off his bulging arm muscles. He looks amazing.

Not that I notice.

He's armed with a yellow notepad, graphing paper, and some sticky notes.

"No laptop?" I ask.

"Nope. I like to draw things out. It's from my drafting days," he says, putting the pencil behind his ear.

"Let's start off with asking you what kind of magazine do you want?"

I think about that. Over the years, it has changed. I went through a short spurt where I fostered kittens for the Humane Society and thought I wanted to start a cat magazine. But there are tons of them already.

When I was running, I wanted to start a runner's magazine, but I already subscribed to *Runner's Life* and it covered most of the topics I could think of.

I can't cook, so a recipe magazine won't work.

I like to read, but "Reader's Magazine?" I think they already have a digest.

Josh can see my indecision. "I want you to fill this out before you think any further," he says, and hands me a questionnaire and a freshly sharpened pencil. "The answers will remain confidential. Only I will see them."

I look at it. It's quite long and comprehensive.

"Can I get you something to drink first?" I ask. "I made coffee. It's decaf."

He laughs. "Sure. That would be great."

While Josh sips his coffee and pets Mouser, I work at filling out the questionnaire.

The first question is:

Do you feel stuck in place and want to move forward but are unsure how to get unstuck?

Ummm....yes. Of course. Although people with lots of money shouldn't have that problem. So I put "NO."

What do you normally do during the day?

I look at the TV. Then my laptop. Then my iPhone. I AM INVOLVED IN SOCIAL MEDIA AND PURSUE CONNECTIONS RELATED TO MY ONGOING WRITING PROJECT.
That sounds about right.

Do you have a difficult time balancing your work, family, and friends?

Well, not really. I don't have a job, or a boyfriend, and most of my friends work at InterFind, a place I'm never setting foot in again.
NO.

Do you know how to release stress?

I look at the stain on the carpet from the empty wine bottle.
YES.

Where on the aliveness index would you place yourself?

There's a line with an arrow pointing left to the *Comfort Zone*, and I read the description. This is the mundane existence of a person who is comfortable but wants more. They have a job, clothes, and family. I skip forward. In the middle is the

Pain Zone. "If you're in the pain zone, you'll know it," says the caption. Off to the right is the *Aliveness Zone.* If I lived there, I obviously wouldn't need a life coach.

Comfort zone, pain zone, aliveness zone. I glance up at Josh. He gives me a large smile. I circle the *Aliveness Zone* and then look back up at him. He's scratching Mouser behind the ears, and the cat's purring. He's not on his phone or acting restless. He looks so relaxed sitting there on my couch, so sure of himself. So peaceful. I erase my circle and boldly circle *Pain Zone.* After all, I am paying this man to help me.

I get up and get myself a glass of water.

"How you doing? Any questions?" Josh asks.

"Nope. Almost done." I sit back down.

What special skills or knowledge do you have?

Oh dear. Here we go again. Well, I can write. WRITING. Although I'm not doing a very good job on this particular assignment. Or my novel. I cringe. I'm definitely in the Pain Zone.

Write down some significant events in your life.

The only thing I can think of is the time in seventh grade when Claudia Sallow and I stole the car of the woman who used to babysit for me and eased it down the street. (Neither of us could drive, obviously.) It got stuck in a ditch, and we had to call the tow truck to get us out. I was grounded for a month.

LEARNING TO DRIVE

The questionnaire goes on to ask about my favorite hobbies, my close friends, my education, etc. I fill it out the best I can. Josh gets up and refills his coffee, offering me some. I shake my head.

Two questions left.

Do you trust easily?

I frown. Definitely not anymore. Especially not lawyers.
NO.

Are you ready to turn your life over to your life coach?

I look up at Josh. Maybe this is it. Maybe this is the start
of my new life. Can I trust this man after I have sworn never
to trust a man again? Why didn't God send me a *woman* life
coach? Oh, what the heck.
YES.
And I hand my paper to Josh.

Chapter Six

We meet the next day at Starbucks. He buys the coffees.

"You didn't put down any interests other than writing," he says. "It's going to be hard for me to help you figure out some goals."

I look down at my coffee cup. "I know. The truth is I'm just not really that good at anything. I'm average. Boring, even."

I can feel him watching me with that steady stare of his, working out what to say.

"I'm not looking for sympathy," I say. "I don't want to come across as pathetic. But don't you think that sometimes we just have to give up trying to be something we aren't?"

"What are you giving up?" he asks.

"Well, men for one thing," I say, and laugh. "I obviously make poor relationship choices."

"Just that once though," he says.

There was also the juggler in high school who ran off to join the circus (literally) after our first date. And the "cowboy" with the sexy hat I met in college who was very sweet, but it turns out he had a hidden addiction to cocaine. I accidently uncovered it one day when I kissed him and powdery dust fell on my nose. Apparently he stored it in his hatband. I had always wondered why his nose ran.

I don't mention those to Josh.

"And I lost my job. They didn't fire me because I'm not good—they fired me because I'm boring."

Josh shakes his head.

"I've gotten two tickets this year."

"So you have a police record," he laughs.

Little does he know.

"I wanted to be a journalist, but wasn't able to land a job when I got out of college. I have a few clippings from an internship, but it's not enough. I tried freelancing for a while before I worked at InterFind, but it just doesn't pay enough right now...and since I'm not experienced, I keep getting rejection letters for articles I send to magazines. I'm just not good enough yet."

"Hey," Josh says.

I look up. His blue eyes look into mine.

"You *are* good enough. You're exactly that, *good enough*. You just don't see it. You help your neighbor out, Mrs. Burgess. She told me all about you the other day when I came to your door. She told me you used to foster kittens until you kept one. The perfect one, you said, and then you quit so it wouldn't happen again. At least you know when to quit."

I'll have to talk to Mrs. Burgess about discussing my private life. I hope she didn't tell him I only fostered that one batch.

"I've only known you for a short time and already I can see that you're smart, funny, pretty, devoted to your family, sincere…all those things are so much more important than you think. You're good enough, Amy. In fact, you're awesome."

Pretty? Did he say I was pretty?

He's serious. He reaches across the table and takes my hands in his, not in a romantic way, but in an "I want you to listen to this because it's important" way.

"You're just going through some tough stuff right now. But I'm going to help you see how really awesome you are, and we're going to plan a life path for you that will make you realize your potential."

I nod. He looks so convincing and he speaks with such conviction that he can make me believe anything.

Gosh, this guy is good at his job!

"Okay," I say quietly. Then, in a stronger voice, "Okay."

"Give me a few days to process things, and when we meet again, we'll come up with a plan for you and maybe figure out what career you're after or what type of magazine you want to start."

I nod, and as we leave the coffee shop, I'm feeling a little better about life.

As I lay in bed that night, I run through my mind all the things Josh said. I think about how I like to help people. About my childhood, how awesome my parents were and are, and how much confidence they have in me. And how my teachers said I'd do well in life. I can't let down all those people who have invested so much into me. I'm blessed, very blessed, and I need to somehow share my blessings with the world. If I can't do that through my job, or through marriage, how can I do it?

I think back to my childhood dream of owning a magazine. Why did I think it was silly? Maybe I can publish a magazine that would help people. But isn't that what most magazines do already? It will have to be really specific.

Suddenly, I have it all figured out. I can't wait until morning when I can tell Josh!

"I know what I want to do with my life!" I shout, probably a little too excitedly, when he answers his phone.

"And what's that?" Josh says. I can hear the smile in his voice.

"I want to start up a magazine. I'm going to call it *Good Enough*, and it's going to be a magazine to empower people. There will be self-help articles, but there will be more than that. I'm going to remind people that they are already good enough! We'll have articles on weight, fashion, meals, parenting, exercise—just like the other women's magazines out there. But the focus will be on knowing when you've done enough, or are enough, or have enough. Maybe we'll even have regular-sized models instead of those really tall, skinny girls, and we'll include healthy restaurants for quick take-out meals because sometimes you really don't have time to cook, and – "

"Wow, hold on!" Josh is laughing. "That sounds like a great idea! I just had a client cancel so I have the morning off. How about I come over now, and we'll write up a plan?"

After I hang up, I practically dance around the apartment. I'm so happy. Nothing in my life has ever felt this right. I finally know what I'm going to do. I'm going to help people. And I have the money to do it.

Chapter Seven

Josh and I write it all down on some yellow steno pads he brings with him. The magazine will be both hard copy and online because while I love my electronics, I prefer to hold a magazine in my hands and leaf through it when I read. Then we come up with categories, like I had told him earlier. Articles we'll write—or hire people to write. I want this magazine to be for women who are tired, searching, working too hard, and trying to wear all the hats that women need to wear. At the end of the day, I want them to be able to pick up this magazine and see that they don't need to improve themselves—that they are already good enough the way they are and most of them are probably going over and above what is expected of them.

You are enough. You do enough. You have enough.

That's going to be my mission statement.

I'm so excited I can hardly sit still.

After we get it all written down, Josh gives me that serious look again.

"Now for the hard part," he says. "We have to come up with some capital."

"Capital?"

"Money. There are going to be start-up costs. I suppose we can probably hire freelance writers who will work for free just to see their name in print, but there will be printing costs, and…"

Josh continues on but my mind wanders. I have money. I have enough money for the building, the printing presses, and the staff.

He opens up his laptop. "Let's do some searches on costs…"

"The money won't be a problem," I say.

He looks up.

"I…I think I might have enough."

He raises an eyebrow. "You don't even have numbers yet."

"Okay. Get me some numbers, and I'll see what I can do."

Then I go home and panic. If I start spending the money, will people notice? My original plan was to sit on it while I hunted for a job and then worked. I'd slowly "save" and then do something big in a few years, like buy a house. In the meantime, I had planned to give some to charity and pay off my parents' mortgage. I hadn't figured out how to do that yet, but I'm sure there would be some contest I could make up for them to win or something.

After pacing around the apartment for several hours, I come up with a plan. I'll start up the magazine under some pretend name and put myself as the Editor. My friends and family can assume I am making big money that way. Only Josh needs to know I'm the owner.

While we're setting up the building and hiring people, I'll tell Mom and Dad that I'm an advisor. No, I don't have the experience for that. I've been contracted out because of my vast experience at InterFind with the writing world. I've been contracted out to make the company writer-friendly like InterFind was.

Yes. That's it.

I sigh and pet Mouser. What have I gotten myself into?

Josh comes back the next day with numbers. They're pretty big. We talked long into the evening yesterday and figured out that I need a building, printing presses, and so much more. He wrote everything down just to make me happy, but he kept shaking his head and smiling, thinking I was shooting for the moon.

"Well, it'll be good to know what I'm getting into," I said.

I look down at the numbers he printed off for me. Prices to buy presses vs. renting. Costs for setting up the business. Going pay rates for freelancers and staffers.

I look at them for a while, pretending to think. Then I look up and say, "Okay."

"Okay what?"

"Okay. Let's get started."

I point at the list of buildings for rent and sale in the area.

"Let's go look at these."

"Those are kind of pricey, and they will only show them to us if we're serious."

"I am serious. I have the money." I sit up taller, trying to look professional in my jeans and V-neck T-shirt. Why hadn't I dressed smarter this morning? Oh yeah. I don't have many clothes.

He sits back, arms crossed, and searches me with those blue eyes of his. "Where did you get that much money?"

He has seen my furniture. And possibly noticed my lack of wardrobe. I smooth my hand down over my jeans.

"Um. Well. I inherited it," I lie.

I was up for a while last night trying to figure out how I was going to explain to Josh that I could afford to finance my plan.

"Your parents are still alive," he says.

"My aunt. Long-lost aunt."

He looks at me for a moment and then looks around my apartment.

"No offense, but you don't live like you have money."

He has obviously seen my car.

"Well, no. It was rather recent that she died."

What am I doing?

"I'm sorry for your loss," he says, and seems to gather himself. "Okay, let me make a few phone calls, and we'll go look at some property."

The third place we see is perfect. It's a three-story brick building, close to downtown, which puts it within walking distance of all the shops and restaurants. The basement is a great place to put printing presses, and the ground floor already has a lobby area and reception desk. Behind that are conference rooms. On the second floor are offices and cubbies for workers (my writers!), and there's a big open room on the third floor where I envision setting up art and photo and fashion. It's classy.

And it's expensive.

Josh doesn't say anything as we set up meetings and sign papers the next day. He does raise an eyebrow when I ask my lawyer if there's a way I can set things up so my name won't be on the building as the owner.

"There is," he says, and it takes us quite a while to do more paperwork. He asks me if I have a name for my DBA, which stands for "Doing Business As." (I'm learning some really cool new terms!) I think and then suddenly it comes to me.

"Second Chances," I say.

The lawyer writes that down. I glance at Josh, who is looking at me with admiring eyes. "Anonymous again, huh?" he says. "Why 'Second Chances?'"

"Because this is my chance at my dream," I say. "I didn't follow it the first time around. And now, here I am."

I mean, after all, I lost my job and my boyfriend and didn't really follow my childhood dream. But now, somehow, here I am, able to do what I really want to do.

I envision helping others. I'll give jobs to people who really need them. I'll start up charities. Maybe I'll foster more kittens.

Josh smiles and reaches across the table to give my hand a little squeeze. His hand is warm, his grip firm. A tingle runs through me at his touch, but then he takes his hand away. Too soon.

Not that I care.

We fill out more paperwork, and I sign about a gazillion things. Then we're done.

Josh has done his homework. After we're through at the lawyer's office, he tells me he's found some professionals in the field to talk to. We figure out what we really need, what are the best brands, and where we should purchase those things. We find a place that is selling used printing presses, and we buy those.

The next day, Andrea takes me out shopping.

"Girlfriend, I don't know what you were thinking when you threw all your clothes out," she says, "but with this fancy new job you're doing as a consultant, we need to get you some clothes."

So we spend the morning going to my favorite clothing stores. I find myself trying on clothes that I think Josh would like to see me in. Turquoise has always brought out my eyes, so I find some tops in that color. Slimming pants. A few skirts. I try to push Josh out of my mind, but I can't. I buy a few pairs of jeans. I do, after all, need to look good on the weekends too.

"Does this bag go with this outfit?" I ask, holding a purse up beside myself while I'm modeling a pair of skinny jeans and a turquoise sweater.

"It's the perfect touch," says Andrea. "But I thought we were looking for office wear."

"I need weekend wear as well," I say, defensively. "Have you seen my closet?"

"As a matter of fact, yes," says Andrea, who was just over last week and nearly had a heart attack at my pared-down wardrobe. So I buy the purse.

After lunch, we head to the shoe store. I find a few pairs of spiky heels in the perfect colors to wear with the clothes I picked out. I throw in some flats and a pair of Nike trainers.

My wardrobe isn't too much wilder than the one I gave away. There are still plenty of sensible colors but they seem perfect for the owner of a magazine, so I'm happy with them.

By the end of the day, I'm exhausted and head home to be alone. I've just settled down on the couch in my new PJs when Josh texts me.

How was your day?

Awesome.

Mine too. Got a new client. He's a chef wanting to start up a yoga and yogurt restaurant.

????

Yes, it's true.

I laugh and send a few fun emots over.

Ready for tomorrow? he texts.

Yep!

Josh has a list of contacts, and I have been writing up ads this week. Tomorrow we're going to put those ads in papers.

And we do. He comes over bright and early, and I just happen to be wearing my casual skinny jeans with my turquoise short-sleeved sweater that Andrea says makes me look "fuller" at the top.

Not that I'm trying to impress Josh, but I do need to look nice. I am, after all, a professional now. He's in his usual comfy jeans, this time paired with a light yellow shirt. I notice that he has a nice, warm tone to his skin.

I've made coffee. (Decaf for him, of course. I still haven't given up the caffeine. Nor do I intend to.) Then we get to work.

Together, we put ads in papers for writers, photographers, and fashion designers. It's time consuming. We work closely over the next few weeks buying equipment and readying the building. My checks clear and nobody comes to arrest me. As for Josh, he never once asks me again where the money is coming from.

It's not so easy with my parents.

"Honey, do you know what you're doing?" asks my dad when I go over for dinner one Sunday.

"Of course!" I say cheerfully.

Everybody has admitted I have never looked happier. I tell them that I'm working with a firm to set up a magazine and they're paying me as a consultant to help get things started. They questioned my consulting experience, but I tell them the people wanted somebody cheap so they were willing to give me a try.

I realize I'm lying to everybody, but I don't know what else to do. Now that I have decided to keep the money, I have to go with the story.

I am also paying Mrs. Burgess's rent. The building owner has agreed to keep it anonymous.

We're so busy I forget all about Bart (okay, mostly) and don't have much time to think about anything other than work. Then one evening after talking about whom we're going to bring in to interview, Josh packs his yellow pads away in his backpack and sits back in his chair. It's actually my chair, but he is over to my apartment so often that it has become, by default, his chair.

"You're working too hard," he says.

I look up from my laptop. I'm entering numbers in an Excel spreadsheet.

"Well, I have to."

"As your life coach, I have to insist on some balance. You need to have fun or you'll burn out."

I frown. "I am having fun."

"Non-work fun," he says. "Close your laptop."

"What?"

"Close your laptop. It's 7:30 p.m. You need to eat dinner."

I think about that. I've been living off microwave meals that I pull out of the freezer at the end of each day.

"There's a great restaurant downtown. Whitman's. It's across the street from your building. You can gaze upon your work as you eat."

I sit back in my chair and look across the table at Josh. "Are you asking me out to dinner?"

He hesitates, but only a little. We've been working so closely these past few weeks that we're comfortable with each other. He has a few other clients, but none that take the time that I've taken. I'm almost exclusively his.

"Yes," he says finally. "Sometimes we take our clients to dinner."

I'm not sure how to take that. As much as I don't want another man in my life, I have to admit that I'm attracted to Josh. He hasn't made any moves to let me think he feels the same way, but there's a look in his eyes when he looks at me.

I'm probably just caught up in all the fun of this whole process. He's just a man I've hired.

"Okay," I say and close my laptop. "Dinner. Let me go get changed." I'm thinking of the navy pants and blouse in the closet. And maybe I could pull my hair back.

"Amy," Josh says in that calm way he has.

I look at him again. "What?"

"You're good enough. Let's go."

I hesitate, but only for a moment. Here's a man who is happy to be with me the way I am. Maybe I need to work on feeling better the way I am too.

"Okay," I say, smiling. And we leave.

Josh drives, and we have to stop by his house first so he can pick up a package he needs to get to another client tonight. He rarely talks about himself, so I don't know much about him. I'm curious to see where he lives.

It's a modest Cape Cod on a side street on the west side of town. It's old, by the looks of the outside. When I step inside, I'm amazed by how clean and neat it is. He has hardwood floors, and the natural-wood-colored banister and moldings are beautiful. Then I see the furniture. The kitchen table, a buffet, and an armoire for the television all look handmade, with precise fittings and beautiful curves. I then remember he once told me he liked to do woodwork.

"Did you make these?" I ask.

"Yes," he says, and smiles. "Just a little side hobby. I did the woodwork in the house too. The floors, banister, and moldings. I enjoy it, and it's a great way to relax."

Wow. It's more than a hobby. He could make a living doing this. It's beautiful.

"You ready?" he says. He has a box in his hands.

"Uh, yes." I let him usher me out to the car, but I can't stop thinking of the beautiful work he does.

He stops at a business and leaves the package inside with a security guard. "He needs that in the morning," Josh says. "I'm helping him with some financial planning and that's something he wanted me to order for him." I often forget that Josh has other clients because we spend so much time together.

Dinner is great. Josh asks the waiter for a table near the window, and we can see my building from where we sit. It's late May now, and the flowering trees along the street are in bloom. But I imagine it in the winter, at Christmas, and remember how beautifully the city decorates.

"We can put a big wreath up there," I say, nodding to an area on the third floor. "And maybe hire someone to hang some pine roping. And we'll put little white lights up." Josh smiles and agrees. He gives me some of his ideas, and it's fun sitting there planning.

It's late when he drops me off at my apartment.

"I had fun," I say, honestly. "Thanks for reminding me to play." He looks at me for a moment and then quietly takes my hand. I think he's about to lean forward and kiss me.

"Amy," he says, giving my hand a little squeeze and letting it go. "I had fun too."

I realize the night is over. I smile, happy inside, because while Josh might not be my boyfriend, he's at least my friend. And that is so awesome. He waits until I unlock the main door and go inside. I stand there for a moment, waving as he drives away. Then I walk up to my apartment to get ready for bed.

That Sunday, my parents take me out to lunch after church.

My brother Tad joins us with his family. Tad is married to Darlene, and she is the most awesome sister-in-law a girl could wish for. They have a new baby, Charlie, which is why I don't see them much anymore. They're always busy and sleep-deprived.

"So who is this man you work with all the time that you want me to meet?" Tad asks. He has stopped by the new building a few times to take me out to lunch, but Josh was always off with another client or something, so I never got to introduce them. I was always bummed they missed each other.

"A new man?" Mom asks curiously. Her brows shoot up.

"He's a life coach," I say. Everyone looks at me for more explanation.

"Well," I begin. Where am I going to go with this? "After I lost my job and my boyfriend..."

"And then tossed all your clothes," Mom adds.

"Yes, that. I figured I needed a new start in life. I thought I'd start over fresh."

"That's why you changed careers from a writer to a consultant!" says Darlene. "I get it now."

"That and she needed a job," Dad says.

"Yes," I say. "So there I was, standing in Starbuck's, and he was in line in front of me. I saw his card, and we started talking."

I pause. I don't want to lie to anybody.

"So..." Tad asks.

"That's it. Just my life coach."

"What's his name?" asks Darlene.

"Josh. Josh Gray." I love the sound of his name as it rolls off my tongue.

"*Josh Gray?*" says Tad. "Is he a construction worker?"

"He was. Now he's a life coach. Do you know him?" I look warily at Tad, who is looking troubled.

"Um...I know *of* him." Tad has worked in construction for years. He designs and builds houses, which is why I wanted him to meet Josh so badly. I thought they'd hit it off well.

I feel the pit of my stomach turn. "And?"

"Nothing," says Tad. "I'm sure it's fine."

"*What's* fine?"

But then the baby starts crying, and Darlene feels his diaper and says he's wet. Tad takes him and the diaper bag off to the restroom. When he gets back, our check comes, and we never get to finish our conversation.

Chapter Eight

The next day, Andrea and I are having lunch together. She has dyed her hair purple, saying it's the new black. She has it cut into a pixie, which looks adorable on her with her big eyes and dark lashes.

I've been telling her all about the building and how the company is going to start hiring soon.

"That must be really cool, being a consultant," she says. "How did you get this job again?"

"My life coach," I say. Which really isn't a lie. If it weren't for Josh, I wouldn't be doing what I'm doing.

"Yes," says Andrea, her eyes narrowing. "You talk about this Josh character an awful lot. Could it be that you have a thing for him?" She smiles.

"No," I say and then feel myself blush. "Well, yes. Maybe. But we work together, so it can never happen. It says right in my contract that life coaches can't have any romantic connections with their clients." I know this because I've read it about a dozen times. Just to be sure.

"You could fire him," Andrea says.

"No!" I say. "We start interviewing soon. I need him."

"So he's like a consultant who is consulting you on consulting," says Andrea. Somehow, that makes sense.

"Yes," I say. She's pretty sharp. I can see she doesn't totally believe my story, but she doesn't push. Then, excitedly I pull my laptop out.

"I've got to show you our—the company's—new website!" I say. There's Wi-Fi in the restaurant, and I pull it up in no time.

"Wow," says Andrea.

I'm so proud of it. It's really sharp and snazzy, and I think it will appeal to our target audience, which is busy women of all ages. "That's so cool, Amy. And really you haven't left the world of writing at all. Do you think this magazine will fly?"

"Of course," I say. Honestly, I haven't figured out what to do if it doesn't. Our food comes, so I put away my laptop.

"How's life at InterFind?" I ask. I miss my coworkers, but I no longer miss my job. We talk for a bit about InterFind and Andrea's boyfriend and other things. Then lunch is over, and we both have to get back to work.

Josh meets me at our new address, 302 W. Orchid. Once again, I realize how much I love the street name. Orchid. It's beautiful, like the building. I'm giddy with excitement and also a little nervous because it's finally time to start interviewing people to hire.

Josh and I have worked so many hours organizing the magazine that I know exactly what I want it to be and have figured out what types of people I need to hire. I'm so glad Josh is here with me. He's good with people, and with his life coach skills, he'll be awesome at helping me interview.

He actually researched interviewing and came up with guidelines for us so we get what we're looking for.

We got tons of resumes from the ads we put out in newspapers, on Craigslist, on LinkedIn and wherever else we could find. We picked the top three in each category and are interviewing people today. Some we've flown in from other states.

I love having money.

The first person is a writer. He's smart, savvy, and quite experienced. Josh said we should hire less-experienced people to save money, but I insisted we get some of the best. I don't want this to fail.

We spend the morning interviewing, and by lunch, my head is spinning.

"Should we order in?" I say, realizing we only have an hour before our next interviewee comes in.

"No, let's get some air," Josh says.

We decide to walk down to the little café around the corner. They have the most amazing sandwiches on homemade Italian bread. I'm thinking about their savory glazed chicken with melted cheese when I see a homeless man sitting up against the building next to the café. He looks to be in his fifties and has long scraggly hair and a beard. He's holding up a sign that says *Will Work for Food.*

As we walk past, he looks up at me with surprisingly sober and very blue eyes. "Can you help me, ma'am?" he says. I smile politely and shake my head as we walk inside to order.

"We should get him something," I whisper.

"I was thinking the same thing," says Josh. He orders two melts and gets two waters. I get my chicken sandwich, and we leave. The man is still there, and Josh hands him the sandwich and one of the waters.

The man takes them and hungrily tears open the wrapper of the sandwich. "Thank you, sir. Thank you," he says, stuffing a big bite into his mouth. I smile, feeling better about life. It feels so good to help someone.

"You're welcome. You have a nice day," says Josh, and smiles at the man. Josh has the kind of face that makes you feel it's going to be okay. Maybe that's what the man grabs on to.

"Sir," he says and quits eating for a moment. His eyes travel to me and then back to Josh. "I used to have a job," he says.

"Oh," says Josh. "What did you do?"

The man tells us he used to put roofs on houses until his back gave out. He lost his business and then his wife and children. His medical bills took their toll, and now here he is. I want to say that the way he's sitting all slouched against the wall isn't helping his back any, but I don't. I can't count the times Mom hollered at us about our posture.

"I tried to find a different job," says the man, "but I don't have no college education."

Then it hits me. Why stop at giving the man a sandwich? Why feed a man a meal when you can teach him to grow food? Or something like that.

"I can offer you a job," I say before I realize it.

"Really?" His face brightens, and he sits up straighter. I'm relieved for his back.

"Really?" Josh echoes, his face quizzical.

"Um, yes." I say.

"Doing what?" says the man.

"Yes, Amy, doing what?" echoes Josh.

I think quickly. We still haven't picked up any janitorial service. "I own a business. How about doing the cleaning? You know, vacuuming, dusting, bathrooms. Stuff like that. Janitorial. Can your back handle that?"

"Ma'am, I'd be thrilled and honored," says the man who begins to stand, reaching his hand out to shake mine. As he does, his coat parts and a liquor bottle rolls out. "Oh," he says, kicking it back with his foot. "I'm not drunk. I don't drink before noon."

"It's noon now," says Josh.

"And I am now going to stay sober, since I have a job," says the man, who starts eating his sandwich again, standing there. "My name is Harlan, by the way."

We shake, and I hand him my card. I tell him that tomorrow is busy, but if he could come the next day, we'll put him to work.

As we walk away, Josh sighs.

"And I thought I was the one fixing people's lives," he says.

"Do you think I did the right thing?" I say. "He could be a drunk or an axe murderer, and I just gave him my name and number."

"He is a drunk, but I doubt he's an axe murderer," says Josh. "Maybe." We get back to the office and sit down in the breakroom with our sandwiches.

"I'm all for giving people a fresh start in life, Amy," says Josh. "But this man...he needs to clean his act up before he starts working here. Clean up his beard. Bathe. Perhaps even get sober. Especially get sober."

I look at him, and we laugh.

"What have I done?" I say.

"You've either just saved a life or brought us a whole lot of trouble," says Josh. "Only time will tell."

That evening, I stop in an engraving store to buy myself a nameplate for my desk. It occurs to me, then, that I have to tell my parents something more about my job. Like the fact that I'll be editor.

And I need to do it before the first issue comes out with my name on it. So I call them. It's easier to lie over the phone. "Mom!" I say. I'm wearing my favorite pajamas and am curled up on the couch with Mouser. She's purring, and I'm scratching her behind the ears. "Guess what?"

"What?" Mom says.

"I applied for the editor job at the magazine, and I got it! Editor, Mom! I'm going to be the EDITOR!"

"Oh, honey, I always knew you would do something amazing! Not that everything you do isn't amazing, but I know how much you love to write!" I love that about her. She always gets so excited for me. Even the time I made fourth chair in fifth grade band—she acted like I had won a place in the Detroit Symphony Orchestra.

I hear her yell the news to my dad, and he picks up the other line.

"It's going to be great," I say. "And this magazine is exactly what I want to do." I tell them all about *Good Enough* and what it means and how it's going to reach all women where they are and help them feel good about themselves. It's going to celebrate women just because we are women.

The conversation goes well, and after I hang up, I'm shaking. I hadn't realized how excited I really was about this whole thing. I've been so worried about hiding the money that I haven't really been able to focus on what I'm doing. I'm living my dream. My dream of starting up a magazine.

Mouser rubs against me, and I realize I've stopped petting her.

"Mouser," I say. "My life has begun."

The next day, we interview more people, and the morning goes by in a blur. By lunchtime, I'm exhausted, thrilled, and excited all at the same time.

"Let's order in," I say.

"Safe choice," says Josh, a twinkle in his eyes. "We don't want you bringing home any more strays."

We order some Chinese take-out and sit in the breakroom, just the two of us.

"Wow," I say. "This is amazing. I really like that one girl for photography. She's so creative. I love her portfolio."

Josh agrees and spears a shrimp with his fork.

"So..." he hesitates. "Amy. Tell me again where this money is coming from. How much did your aunt leave you exactly?"

I gave Josh a budget last week. He hasn't asked me again about my finances since I told him the lie about inheriting it from my aunt. I look guiltily down at my plate. Josh has become my best friend over the past few months. I care about him a lot. I don't want to lie to him.

"Why don't you not ask me about the money," I say.

"Why are you still living in your apartment and driving that little car if you have millions of dollars?" He pauses. "You don't have to answer that. I guess I'm just really awed by you, Amy, every time I think about it. You have all of that money, yet your main goal is to create this magazine in order to try to make people feel better about themselves. And when I talked to Mrs. Burgess the other day, she told me someone was anonymously paying her rent." He squinted. "Could that be you?"

"It's anonymous for a reason," I say.

"I'm sorry," he apologizes again and spears another shrimp. Then he looks back up at me. "Amy, you're the most amazing person I've ever met."

There's a silence between us at the table as we meet each other's eyes. I don't know what to say. I've stolen a lottery ticket from my ex-boyfriend. I've lied about it to everybody I know. I still think hateful things about the woman he cheated on me with. How can I be amazing? I'm a coward, a bully. I'm horrible.

But Josh's blue eyes are watching me. Just being with him makes me feel like I'm okay. Like I'm a better person. I don't want this feeling to leave. I realize then how I've grown to feel about him.

"And you're the most amazing person I've ever met," I say quietly.

Then the buzzer sounds on the door.

"That's our next interview!" I say, and we both jump up.

"Go," says Josh. "I'll put this in the fridge."

It's a woman about my age. She's smartly dressed in a navy blue pin stripe suit with a white blouse underneath and navy heels. Her long, auburn hair is pinned up in a neat updo that shows off her diamond earrings. She has amazing green eyes.

"Hi," she says, extending her hand. "I'm Suzanne."

Her voice is soft, small, and doesn't really match her suit. But her handshake is firm.

Josh joins us in the conference room.

Suzanne is here to interview for the administrative assistant job. She lives about an hour away, but is willing to move closer. Her resume isn't all that impressive, but when I talked to her on the phone, she sounded so excited about the job that Josh and I decided to interview her since we didn't have to pay to fly her in. She has had some temp jobs since college, but she hasn't worked for the past two years. When I called her references from the temp jobs, they all loved her.

After asking her some basic questions, I asked why she hasn't worked in the past two years.

"I had a baby," she said. "I was planning to stay home and take care of him, but my husband and I separated and..." She gives a little laugh. "I really need a job."

My heart goes out to her. Obviously, she had some money previously because her clothes and diamond earrings tell me that. I glance at Josh.

"We have two other people to interview for this job," he says. "Then we'll let you know."

"Wait," says Suzanne. "I'll work hard. I'll work overtime. Your ad says you have on-site childcare, and I'd love to be at a place where I don't have to be far from my son. Honestly, I've been on several interviews, but because of my background, I'm not qualified for much. Just give me a chance. I won't let you down."

There's determination in her eyes. I like this woman. I glance at Josh.

"We'll let you know," he says.

After she leaves, I turn to Josh.

"I really want to hire her," I say. "That's what this magazine is about. Helping people. Letting her know she's good enough. I think we should give her a chance."

"I do too," Josh says. "But we have to at least interview the others first. It's only fair."

We do, and fortunately, they aren't as impressive. They may have better resumes but their personalities are a bit harsh. One woman was very demanding about vacation time and had even brought the dates she needed off next year.

So it's settled. We hire Suzanne, and she's to start the following Monday. We spend the rest of the day filling most of the writing spots and put together a nice creative team for ads, graphics, and photos.

By the end of the week, we have a fashion designer, a chef and a psychologist on our staff as consultants. And Harlan showed up sober for his job. I'm so excited.

It's Friday evening and I'm exhausted. Josh and I have worked late interviewing. It's nearly 8 p.m., and I haven't eaten since lunch.

As I pack up my laptop, Josh comes into my office. "It was a good day," he says. He's standing there, with his hands in the pockets of his blue chinos and his soft cotton shirt falling down over his muscular shoulders. He is so handsome. His dark, curly hair is a bit long because he hasn't had time for a haircut.

I zip up the case of my laptop bag, set it aside, and walk over to Josh. I give him a friendly hug. "Thanks so much for everything," I say.

He takes my hands in his, "Amy," he says and pulls me closer. I can smell his aftershave. I close my eyes.

I feel his breath on my face. Then he pulls back.

"I have to go," he says.

What? I open my eyes.

"It's late," he says. "I have another client in the morning. I've been neglecting my other clients so we could get the interviewing done, but now I think I can step back a little bit. I'll see you on Monday, okay?"

"Um, okay," I say. I was just about to ask him if he wanted to get some dinner. Clearly NOT.

His eyes search mine for a moment, but I turn away and grab my jacket. "I'm starved," I say, forcing a smile. "I'm heading home for some food. I'll see you on Monday."

He walks out ahead of me and holds the door open. I lock up the building. He walks me to my car.

"Good night," he says and then turns and walks down the sidewalk toward where he's parked. I watch him get in and drive away, and then the tear that had been threatening escapes down my cheek. Why did I expect more? Why did I let myself fall for him? I hate men. All men. He's a nice guy, a friend, but that's it. Get a grip, Amy. Love is not in the air for you.

And why do I need love? I have everything a girl could want. Money, my own dream business, and a very nice cat.

With that, I put my little car into gear and drive home.

I knock on Mrs. Burgess's door, and she opens. "Oh, hi, Amy!" she says. She always seems so happy to see me, and it makes me smile.

"Hi, Mrs. Burgess," I say and hand her the mail. I also hand her a bag of canned tuna.

"Thank you, honey," she says. "Would you like to come in for some tea?"

I would, so I do. Her apartment is back to normal, and so is she. I sit down at her kitchen table, kick my shoes off, and curl my feet up under me.

"So are you ever going to tell me about this handsome man I've seen you with so much?" she asks as she puts a kettle of tea on. She has never asked me about Josh before. I guess I should have been the one to bring him up. I'm sure she wonders.

"He's just a co-worker," I say. "Somebody I'm working with on this magazine I told you about."

"Oh?" She turns and raises an eyebrow.

I sigh and run my hands through my hair. "He's really nice, Mrs. Burgess, and I do wish it were more than work, but it's not. He has made that clear."

"Are you sure about that?" she asks. "The way he looks at you."

"That's what I thought," I say. "But tonight, well, tonight I thought things were moving forward, and they very clearly are not."

The teakettle whistles, and Mrs. Burgess pours me a cup. "Decaf," she says. "Since it's so late. Have you eaten?"

"No," I say. "I wanted to ask him out to dinner, but he had to go."

"I have some lasagna in the fridge. Let me heat it up."

Mrs. Burgess's lasagna is the world's best. I sit there and let her fix it for me. She slices some bread to go with it, and puts the butter on the table.

"This is better than a restaurant," I say. Sitting there in her kitchen, feeling warm and loved, I mean those words. Mrs. Burgess never assumes and never pushes. I can just sit and be, and she'll let me.

We make small talk, and when I go home, I'm feeling a lot better. I remind myself that I still have Josh as a friend, a very good friend, and I am thankful.

Chapter Nine

Until I see him the next day, sitting across from a very attractive blonde in a café.

I'm walking down Fourth Street from where I parked, heading over to the homeless shelter, when I see them. They're laughing and talking over breakfast, and he's looking at her with that deep look that I thought he only had for me. Those eyes of his, penetrating hers, and he's giving her that look that says he can fix her life.

At least that's what it looks like from across the street.

All I know is that it hurts and I'm angry. I want to let this go and just be friends, but I can't. I just can't. So I turn and walk on, my step heavy and my face in a frown. By the time I get to the homeless shelter, I've once again banned men from my life. Or at least my love life. I don't need them.

I walk in and am greeted by a smiling woman in her thirties. It's warm outside, so the shelter is nearly empty.

"I'm here to see Harlan," I say.

"Oh, you must be Amy," she says. She leads me down a hallway and into a room with tables and chairs. It looks like a cafeteria. Harlan is sitting on one of the chairs, playing a game of solitaire. On his first day in the office, we interviewed him and told him that he'd have to clean up his appearance a little bit. So he did. He's sitting there with his beard trimmed and his hair shorter. I've brought him some clothes in the sizes he said he wore, and I hand them to him. I got them at the men's shop down the street.

"Hello, Amy!" Harlan says and stands up and reaches for my hand. When I feel his warm grasp, I'm sure I've done the right thing. He thanks me for the clothes and goes to try them on. When he comes back, he looks like something close to handsome.

"Wow, Harlan, you clean up well," I say.

We sit and talk about his duties and what time I expect him to start.

As I leave, I see my parents across the street. "Amy!" Mom exclaims. She waves and runs across the street, jaywalking. Dad glances for cars and follows her. We exchange hugs. "So you're volunteering at a homeless shelter on Saturdays?" Mom says. "That's so awesome."

"We're so proud of you," Dad says and beams.

"I, uh, sort of," I say. "One of the janitors at the magazine, he...I just..." I cut off when I see Josh waving. The blonde isn't with him, and he cuts across the street to join us.

"Amy!" he says, flashing me that smile of his. "What are you doing here? I thought you'd take the day off and rest from our busy week!"

"Hello," says Mom, thrusting her hand out.

"Josh, these are my parents, Herb and Gladys." Josh shakes their hands. "This is Josh Gray. The man I told you I'm working with to set up the magazine."

Everybody smiles and shakes hands.

"I'd love to hear more about this magazine," says Mom. "Amy hardly talks about it, and it's consuming so much of her time."

"That's funny," says Josh. "That's all she talks about when I'm around her." He looks at me and smiles. "You should be so proud of her." He puts a friendly arm around me and I shrug it off, remembering I'm mad at him. Then it dawns on me where this conversation is going. Mom and Dad think I'm just a consultant. Josh thinks my aunt died and I inherited money. I hadn't intended for them to meet yet. Oh gosh.

"Well," I say a little too loudly. "I've got a busy day. Let's move on."

Mom glances at her watch. "Yes, Herb and I have to get to the gym. We have a hot yoga class."

My parents have this new gym membership, and they get to try out different classes free. Before the hot yoga, it was water aerobics. I can't remember the last time I exercised. My parents are probably in way better shape than I am.

"Hot yoga," says Josh. "That sounds interesting. One of my previous clients did that and said she burned tons of calories each session."

"But I'd love to hear more about this magazine," Mom says. "Why don't you come to dinner tomorrow with us? I've invited Amy and her brother. We haven't talked to our daughter for a while. You two can fill us in."

Mom is always inviting people over. Last year she invited our waitress from Pizza Kitchen over for dinner to show her how to make proper antipasto. They hit it off and had a great time.

"No," I say at the same time Josh says "Yes." Josh and my parents both look at me.

"I mean, um, that would be great," I say. "I meant no, I can't talk about this right now. I've really gotta get going."

"Amy's right," Mom says. "Call her later to get directions. Dinner is at 5. Come on, Herb. We're going to be late."

Josh looks at me. "I don't think I can make it tomorrow," he says, in that knowing sense that he has. I smile, relieved.

"Maybe next time," Mom says. She grabs Dad's arm, and they leave.

"I'm sorry," I say. "I'll call you later!" I say as I head back toward my car.

"Amy!" Josh says. I stop, and he catches up. "Are you mad at me or something?"

"Josh, I've gotta go."

"It's just the way you threw my arm off of you. I do realize that was inappropriate behavior from me; you are my client. I'm sorry. And you don't want me to go to dinner. Am I coming across too strongly? Last night...I...I'm sorry."

I'm not sure what he's apologizing about. Almost kissing me and then not, or that he almost kissed me at all.

"Who was that blonde?" I ask before I can stop myself.

"What blonde?" he says.

"The one you were having breakfast with this morning. I saw her on my way to the shelter."

Josh looks startled for a moment but recovers. "Oh, her. That's Clarabelle. She's a client. That's all. Nothing more. I told you, I can't date clients. And even if I could, she's not my type."

"Oh," I say.

"Why?"

I swallow. "I don't know. Just last night, I thought..."

I don't want to continue. If I tell him how I really feel, I could lose him forever. If he doesn't feel the same way, he'll think I'm some stalker client. "I've got to go." I unlock my car, get in, and close the door. I smile and wave, promising to call him again. Then I drive off.

Unfortunately, we have to meet tonight to finalize some things for Monday. So we get together around 5 p.m. at the office.

"Okay, here's our list of who starts on Monday," I say, pulling it out. Then we get out our one-year and five-year plans and go over them together to be sure I'm ready to lead my first meeting on Monday. Josh will be there; he has promised. I'm pretty nervous and pretty excited at the same time. He doesn't mention the awkwardness of our afternoon conversation with my parents.

I get caught up in the work and forget for a while how close he is. Every now and then, our arms accidently touch at the table.

We finally finish at 7 p.m. I stand up, gather up the papers, and put them back in their proper files in my office. I make sure I have everything in place for Monday because I don't want to come in tomorrow.

I pull my coat on, and when I turn to go, there's Josh, standing there. We've turned off most of the lights and there's only the soft light of my desk lamp on him. He's leaning against my office doorframe, his arms crossed, watching me. He smiles.

"How long have you been there?" I say.

"A few minutes."

He walks over to me and fixes the lapel on my coat. Then he takes my hands in his. I swallow.

He starts to say something, and then stops.

"Josh..."

"Amy, I know how you feel about me," he says.

Here it is. He's going to dump me. I gave up men for a reason. I start to pull my hands away from him, but he pulls me in closer. Gosh, he smells good. He rests his forehead against mine. His breath is sweet, like peppermint. He pulls back, and lifts his hand to brush a lock of my hair behind my ear. Then he meets my eyes with those amazing eyes of his. "I can't date clients," he says simply. "I'll lose my job. Company rules."

"Oh," I say. Of course, I already know this. "Well, what if I fire you?"

He smiles. "You don't really need me anymore," he says.

"I need you more than you realize," I say, surprising myself with my directness. He must like it, though, because he pulls me closer to him again.

"So fire me," he says in a whisper.

"You're fired," I say. He moves in toward me, and I close my eyes as our lips meet. It's as wonderful as I've dreamed it would be. I feel like I'm floating. He puts an arm around me, pulls himself against me, and kisses me more.

"I'm out of a job," he mumbles, and we both start laughing. I pull back and look into his eyes. "Amy, I've wanted to do that since the day I met you," he says.

"You have?"

"Yes! You're the most incredible woman I've ever met. I meant it when I said you were awesome. And beautiful."

He kisses me again.

"Let's go to dinner," says Josh. And this time, it really is a date.

Chapter Ten

So on Sunday I bring Josh to dinner at my parents.

I've thought the whole magazine thing over a lot. (I didn't sleep last night I was so stressed.) So I've decided to keep it simple. As we get out of the car, I casually say "Oh, don't mention me owning the magazine or anything. We prefer to think of me as more of a consultant." Then I flip my hair back and close the car door.

"What?" He's not following me. Shoot. I was hoping this would be easier. "Why?"

I stop. He's standing by the car.

"Um…because." Think fast, Amy. "Because we don't like to discuss money at the table." I cringe. I hate lying to him.

He squints at me but lets it go and doesn't ask anything else.

We're having fun and laugh a lot. The magazine doesn't come up during dinner because I have kept my parents busy discussing their new gym classes and the Smiths, who are coming over the following Tuesday for dinner. The Smiths are their best friends and have apparently planned a trip to Italy, which we get to hear about in great detail. So that covers dinner conversation.

I start to relax. I can tell Mom loves Josh immediately and whispers it to me when we go into the kitchen to bring out dessert.

"Amy, he's hot!" she says.

"Mom!" I say, but I'm pleased. It's true. Josh is hot.

"And he seems so nice," Mom adds.

I take out the peach cobbler while Mom brings out vanilla ice cream. Josh accepts a big piece and then Dad asks him how he picks clients to work with.

"I look for two things," he says. "A desire to change and integrity. I think integrity is important. If a client is going to take advantage of another person to fulfill their goals or walk over somebody else, I drop them. Honesty and integrity are important in this world, and they are so undervalued."

I stop eating, my spoon halfway to my mouth. Honesty. Integrity.

"So is that why you took on Amy as a client?" Dad beams. "Amy has always been a good girl. I was so mad at that last bloke who lied to her..."

"Herb!" hisses Mom. "Don't discuss old boyfriends."

Josh laughs easily, unoffended. "I knew I could work with Amy right away. She was ready for a change and had this spark in her eye when we talked about her dreams. She told me she's wanted to start up a magazine since she was a little girl," he says.

"She used to cut out articles and photos from my old magazines and put them together to create her own," Mom says.

"Mom!" I say.

"And she's so kind," Josh says. "She helps out her neighbor by picking up her cat food and getting her mail–did she tell you that? And she's using her wealth to help others by starting up this magazine instead of buying fancy cars or clothes." He gives my shoulder an affectionate squeeze.

"Her wealth?" Mom and Dad echo, and I feel my heart quicken.

"Yes," Josh says. "That's amazing that her aunt—"

Just then, Tad opens the back door. "Sorry we're late!" he says, and he and Darlene spill into the kitchen with a diaper bag, a baby carrier, and a crying Charlie. "He didn't nap, and Darlene was trying to get him down. But as you can see, he's a mad baby."

Darlene unstraps him and picks up the crying infant. He nuzzles into her neck and stops crying.

"He just wants to be held," she says, standing behind her chair and swaying. Tad cuts himself a piece of cobbler.. "What did I miss?"

"Tad, you should eat some dinner first," Mom says, but Tad just globs on some ice cream.

Josh holds out his hand and introduces himself. Tad shakes it. "I've heard about you in the construction world," Tad says.

"Tad owns a construction company," I explain.

"Yes, I used to do that before I became a Life Coach," says Josh. He shakes Darlene's hand too.

Darlene catches my eye and nods her approval. "Cute," she mouths when Josh isn't looking.

I smile, but I'm nervous inside. I pray that the discussion about "my wealth" doesn't come back up.

"Do you miss construction?" Tad asks.

"Not really," says Josh, and takes another huge bite of cobbler.

"I heard you were really good. Won some awards for design," Tad continues, eyeing Josh. "Why–"

Josh cuts him off. "They're no big deal. I'm really happy with my new career. Did Amy tell you that we hired all of her magazine staff?"

Tad says "They were *too* a big deal–"

It's not like Tad to push. What is he doing?

"No," says Josh, more firmly. "They weren't."

What is going on?

Darlene must sense the tension too, because she changes the subject. "So, Amy, tell us about that magazine staff!" she says brightly.

"Um, we hired…well, everybody!" I laugh. "We're all done. We open for business on Monday."

"Aren't you proud of your daughter?" says Josh. "Owning her own magazine and all."

He wasn't supposed to say that!

I choke on a sip of water I was drinking. It goes down the wrong tube, and I start coughing so violently I get tears in my eyes.

Mom jumps up to pat me on the back.

"I'm okay," I manage to choke out. I wave her off and dab my eyes with my napkin.

"Oh my gosh, look at the time," I say, my voice hoarse. "Josh and I have to go."

"What?" Josh looks confused.

"That thing. That thing we have to do." I get up and push my chair back. I quickly kiss Dad on the cheek. "So sorry to run." I kiss Mom's cheek and smile at Tad and Darlene. Josh gets up, quickly eating the last bite of cobbler from his plate as he's standing.

"It was nice meeting you," he says and holds out his hand. They shake hands all around the table. I already have my shoes on and am pulling his arm. When we get in the car, he turns to me. "What was that about? What happened in there?" He says. He looks hurt.

"I told you not to mention me owning the magazine," I hiss.

He looks at me, realization dawning. "I forgot," he says, and I believe him. "Do they not know?"

"No," I say. I'm about to tell him about the lottery ticket. Then I remember what he said about honesty and integrity. What if I tell him and he breaks up with me? What if he says I need to give it all back? We're supposed to open on Monday. What will happen to all these people we hired? They need jobs! What about Homeless Harlan? "I want to surprise them," I say. "When we get the first issue out, I'll tell them. I...I just wanted it to be a surprise," I lie.

Oh, they'll be surprised all right. But this gives me time to think. And I've set the company up under the ownership of a company name, not a person, so nobody can trace it to me without some work. Nobody like Bart. Or my parents. I sigh. What a mess.

"I guess that makes sense," he says.

"So what about those awards you won? Why didn't you want to talk about those?"

"They weren't a big deal," he says. "I don't like attention like that."

"But what were they for?

"I told you, not a big deal," he says, with an edge to his voice that I haven't heard before.

We drive home in silence, and he lets me off at my apartment. "Can I walk you in?" he says.

"No," I say. "I'm tired. I'll see you tomorrow."

We sit there for a minute, and then he leans over and softly kisses me on the lips.

"I'm sorry," I say.

"Me too," he says. Then I get out of my car and head into my lonely apartment. I have to do laundry to get ready for tomorrow morning and the first day of running a working magazine.

Chapter Eleven

I arrive early, before everyone else, and let myself in my building. *My building.* To begin my first day. I stand in my doorway and luxuriate over those words for a moment and then head for my office.

In the dark, I trip over something and then realize that it's a body. It's leaning up against the wall just inside the door, legs protruding across the entrance. I scream at the top of my lungs.

"Humph," it mumbles just as I flick on the light. It's Homeless Harlan, passed out drunk just inside the front door.

Josh pushes his way in, pepper spray in his hand.

"What on earth..." he says and then sees Harlan. He gives me a look.

"What?" I say defensively. I mean, I *thought* he was sober. How can this be my fault?

"Are you okay?" Josh asks, always the gentleman.

"Yes," I say. Josh had agreed to meet me here early so we could open up together and greet everyone. Yesterday, I had ordered flowers for the front office and left a small package of chocolates on each person's desk with little "welcome" cards.

Josh and I look at Harlan. "What are we going to do with him?" I ask. Harlan is snoring, a mop still in his hand. I glance around. "The place is spotless. At least he did his job before he...uh..."

"Yeah, help me move him," Josh interrupts. Josh grabs Harlan under the arms and I grab his feet. We carry him over to the reception desk, where Josh hauls him up into the chair. Harlan is still sleeping.

"Do you think he's okay?" I ask, looking at him. He now has a bit of drool down his chin.

Josh gives me a dark look, which can only mean, "I told you so." "Let's call the shelter to see if somebody will come and pick him up," he says.

While Josh makes phone calls, I turn on lights. The place looks so nice. It's 7:30 a.m., and people will be arriving soon, since we start at 8 a.m. I wander into my office, turn on the light, and sit in my chair for a moment. Then I open my bag, pull out my nameplate, and set it on my desk. It says *Amy Summers, Editor.* I'm the editor! I laugh aloud, unable to contain my glee, and then hear the bell signaling that somebody else has arrived. I hurry out.

Suzanne is standing in the doorway, a baby on her hip. The daycare director isn't here yet.

"What is *that?*" Suzanne says, pointing her other arm, which is loaded with a diaper bag, a purse, and a coffee, in Harlan's direction.

"That's Homeless Harlan," says Josh.

"Harlan," I say. "Maybe if you didn't refer to him as "homeless" he wouldn't be in this mess. You become what you think you are."

"But he is," Josh says, putting his phone away.

"He's in my chair," says Suzanne. "Drooling."

"Uh, yes," I say, and move forward to take Suzanne's bags. "Welcome! We'll have Harlan out of your chair in just a few minutes." I raise my eyebrows at Josh.

"It turns out the shelter doesn't pick up their own," says Josh. "The homeless are expected to get there on the power of their own two feet."

"That's unfair," I say. "I mean, what if he was handicapped? What if he wasn't *able* to walk?"

"He clearly isn't," says Josh.

"Well, heeeeellllllo!" says Bernie, our new daycare director. She waltzes in, all cheery, and smiles at Suzanne and the baby. "Here's our youngest, little Marcus!" she says and holds out her arms. Suzanne gives Marcus a hug and kiss and hands him over. He must only be a few months old. "We'll meet you there, Momma," says Bernie, and whisks off down the hall, not even noticing Harlan. "Oh, heeeeeelllllo, Amy!" She waves her hand behind her.

"Hi!" I shout after her, cheerily. I can be cheery too.

Josh hauls Harlan up out of Suzanne's chair and settles him back on the floor against the wall. "I'll call a cab," he says.

By 10 a.m., everyone has arrived, oooohed and aaaahhed, and eaten their boxes of chocolates. We all assemble in the meeting room. Josh has loaded Harlan into a cab and sent him back to the shelter.

I'm so excited. I have been going over what I am going to say for days, practicing in front of the mirror every night at home. I'm pumped, and I bring up my Power Point and go over the foundation of the company and what it stands for.

We talk about the different sections of the magazine and what I expect in terms of length and substance from the writers. (I've spoken to several editors and writers and this is what I came up with. Plus I read a few good books like *Being a Successful Manager* and stuff like that. You can learn almost anything from a book.)

When I'm done, everybody seems happy and ready to begin.

I walk back to my desk and see a vase of flowers from Mom and Dad with a card that says "Congratulations, Amy! We are so proud of you!"

Josh comes in and closes the door. He gives me a high five, and then we hug. He leans in for a kiss. Just as I'm wanting another one, there's a knock on my door.

"Duty calls," says Josh. "And I have to get back to *my* job. How about dinner tonight?"

"I'd love that," I say. We open the door, and it's Suzanne. She's carrying a yellow steno pad and pen.

I have asked her to meet with me this morning so we can go over her duties. The truth is I'm not sure what all I need her to do at the moment other than answer the phone, file, and make sure everybody is happy.

"How's it going?" I ask.

"Well, the first three hours have been great," she says and beams me a smile. "And I just got back from breastfeeding little Marcus. This is sooooo awesome, having a daycare facility here." She yawns, and then covers it with her hand. "Sorry! He still gets up a lot at night."

"So where is Marcus's dad?" I ask. "Or, really, it's none of my business."

Suzanne sighs and sets her notebook down. "No. It's okay. He left us shortly after Marcus was born." She frowns. "He lied to me so much. I thought he was the greatest thing ever. I worked in a law firm–that's the job I left off my resume–those two years I listed that I wasn't working. Sorry. He was this hotshot lawyer, and he went out of town to help underprivileged people in Detroit, pro bono. He'd be gone for days and then come back. He was a good guy. Or I thought he was." She sighs again.

"Then when Marcus was born and we found out he had cerebral palsy, he said he wasn't ready for this. That it was too much reality. And he left. Just like that. So I'm getting child support from him, but we weren't married or anything, so..." She trails off. "He kept promising to marry me. I even had a ring. I was really stupid."

"What about your parents?"

"They disowned me when I got pregnant. They said I was a slut." She gives a little laugh. "Can you imagine? In this day and age?"

"So you're okay financially, then?" I ask. I can't imagine having a baby with special needs and being all alone.

"Mostly," she says. "I need to work, but all of Marcus's needs will be met. I hope." She frowns again. "You want to know what the worst thing is? I had bought a lottery ticket before he was born. And the numbers won. But I lost the ticket."

Wait. *What?*

"You lost it?" I say.

"Yes. I bought it when I was with my boyfriend. He thought it was silly and made fun of me, saying that lotto's only for the desperate lower class, not for those of us with real jobs. Because I worked in his big, fancy office at the time and was making good money. But I bought it because I thought it would be fun, and I put the baby's due date as some of the numbers. Turns out he was born on his due date!" She smiles for a moment. Then frowns again. "I wish I knew where it was. I looked and looked. My boyfriend only laughed. He said it wasn't important. But he left me."

I hardly hear what she's saying because my mind is churning with thoughts. She lost a lottery ticket.

"Where'd you buy it?"

"The Quick Mart Pump and Pay."

Oh my gosh. That's where I found mine. I'm afraid to ask, but I do.

"What was your boyfriend's name?" I ask as casually as I can.

"Bart."

I'm too stunned to speak. It's her. It's the woman who broke my boyfriend and me up. She's the "other" woman! The woman he bought the ring for.

And it's her ticket, not Bart's!

I squint at her, wondering why she doesn't look familiar. She had blond hair when I saw her with Bart. Obviously, she's changed it. And I only saw the side of her face.

"What did you do at the law office?" I ask. "When you worked with him."

"I was his secretary," she said. "Typical story, huh? Pathetic of me."

I feel my face getting red. I've got to get her out of here. Quickly. I grab my cell phone and pretend to poke some buttons.

"Suzanne, I've got to deal with something," I say, "Something has come up. We'll need to talk later."

"Oh, okay," Suzanne says and gets up. "I'm sorry. I've talked too much about my personal life."

"No, it's okay," I say, escorting her to the door. "This is an emergency. I need to take this."

I give her a little push out the door and close it. Then I close the little shade on the side window so no one can see inside my office and sit down.

She's the "other woman." I've hired the woman who destroyed my happily-ever-after, and I'm working with her.

And...it's her lottery ticket. Not Bart's. *Hers.* I have created a magazine and a life with the money of this woman, who obviously has no idea who I am.

What am I going to do?

Chapter Twelve

This is supposed to be the best day of my life. The day I start my magazine dream. I look at the vase of flowers from my parents. And then at the nameplate on my desk. This is all a sham.

All of it. I've started a business with Suzanne's money.

I guess that's a great get-even story.

The phone rings. "Sorry to bother you," Suzanne says. "It's the woman who runs the homeless shelter. She sounds upset."

I sigh. "It's okay. Put her through."

"Hi, Amy," the woman says when I answer. "Could you come down and see Harlan? He was so upbeat, and we were amazed at the change in him since you hired him. Now he's afraid he has lost his job."

"Well, he did come in drunk," I say.

"And he would like to talk to you about that. Can you come down? He's supposed to go back to work at 5 p.m. tonight, and he's not sure you want him."

I'm silent for a moment.

"He's really sorry," the woman says.

"Okay. Tell him if he shows up sober, he can come in. I'll stick around and talk to him then."

I hang up and look at my flowers again. This day is not going well at all.

Then Suzanne buzzes me. "Your lunch date is here," she says when I pick up.

Darn! I forgot I had asked Andrea to meet me here for lunch to celebrate. I grab my bag and coat and rush down to the lobby. "Hi!" I say a little too happily.

"How's it going?" says Andrea, looking around the place. "You need to have a grand opening party or something. This place is fantastic!"

"I will. Soon!"

The truth is, Josh wanted me to do that this past weekend, but since I'm lying to half of my friends and family, I put it off. I grab Andrea's elbow and try to rush her out. I've got to have time to think. *Think*, Amy!

Memories swirl through my mind. Of Bart breaking up with me. Of the lies he told me for who knows how long. Of the woman on his arm at the gas station. The very pregnant woman.

Suzanne.

"Amy!" Andrea says, shaking me off. "What's the rush? I want to see the place!"

I haven't shown it to her yet, and she's been bugging me for weeks. I had wanted it to be perfect first. Now, I just want to get out of the building.

Andrea puts her hands on her hips and looks me up and down. "Hmmm," she says. "You need to talk."

"Yes," I whisper urgently, because Suzanne is right there. *Right there*, at her desk. I glance at her, but she's busy filing. I briefly remember this morning, just a few hours ago, when my biggest problem was a drunken Harlan in her chair.

"Okay," Andrea says. She knows me well, and she's quick to pick up on things, so she turns to leave. I follow her and don't say a word until we get about a block down the street.

"Okay, spill," says Andrea. She presses the button on her key and unlocks her car. I get in and close the door, leaving the world outside. Andrea climbs in behind the wheel and turns to me. "Spill."

I sigh, deciding how much to tell her.

"You know that awesome office manager I hired?"

"The competent one?" says Andrea. We've both had experiences with incompetent co-workers in our past. She nods knowingly.

"She's the other woman," I say, almost in a whisper.

"The other woman?" Andrea is confused, I can tell. "As in, the other woman besides the one you were going to hire but didn't? I thought she was the only one you wanted to interview because you liked her right away."

"No!" I say. "The *other* woman. As in the woman who broke Bart and me up. The one he was seeing on the side."

Andrea narrows her eyes. "Oh," she says. "The *other* woman."

"Yes!"

Then it dawns on her. "Oh my gosh, Amy! You've got to get her out of there. What's she doing? Spying? Is she there to ruin your life again? Your job? How did you not KNOW?"

"I didn't know because I never really saw her, and I didn't know her name. And when I saw her with Bart that one time, I only caught her profile and she had blond hair then. Obviously from a bottle because it's brown now."

"Does she know who you are?"

"No! She has no idea."

"How do you know?"

I think about the lottery ticket. Suzanne would have never shared that with me if she knew who I was. She trusts me. She has no idea.

"I just know. By some things she said."

"Well, you have to get rid of her."

"But she's good. She's already organized the files and is great at forwarding calls."

It was true. Suzanne had come in on Saturday to set up the filing system and have it ready for today.

"She's alone. Bart left her too. And she has a baby."

"A baby? I can't see Bart leaving you for a woman with a baby." She stops, abruptly. "How old is this baby?"

"Four months."

I could see Andrea doing some quick mental calculations. "It's Bart's baby."

"Yes."

"HE GOT THE OTHER WOMAN PREGNANT WHILE HE WAS STILL DATING YOU?"

I'm glad, then, for the thick glass on the car windows, but a few people walking down the street still turn to look. Andrea can be loud when she's upset.

"Yes," I say. The utter humiliation of it all comes back to me again. How could I have not known? How could I have been so stupid?

We both sit quietly for a moment and think.

"When did you find this out?" Andrea says after a moment.

"Just before you walked in."

"Wow. No wonder you looked so shell-shocked when I saw you."

Andrea turns the car on. "Well, let's get some lunch. And this calls for some heavy duty chocolate for dessert."

We eat at Roadside, my favorite place. I get a double-decker turkey club and order their double chocolate brownie for dessert. A whole piece, not just a half like I usually get.

Andrea digs into her apple berry cobbler with ice cream. "I love it when one of us is stressed," she says.

Under stress is the only time Andrea allows herself to eat sugar. Which means Andrea is under stress frequently, or so she says. But I never mention this to her.

"If I keep her there, I can find out what happened and what's going on with Bart," I say.

"Amy, I'm not sure that's a great idea. Sometime or other, it's going to come up. Won't it stress you to see her every day? I mean, this is the woman who ruined what you thought was your engagement night."

I think about that for a moment. I've had far more fun with Josh than I ever did with Bart. And if we hadn't broken up, then would I have found the lottery ticket and be here today, the first day of my ownership of a new magazine?

"Oh!" I say. "Josh kissed me."

"No!" says Andrea. "What was it like?"

I blush and tell her how much I like him. And it's true. He's so amazing.

"So you're not really missing Bart."

"Not so much," I say.

"But still..."

"I know," I sigh. I wish I could tell her about the lottery ticket. I have to figure out this whole mess. And soon.

I get back, and by this time, I have my game face on. I can handle this. They say it's good to keep your enemies close. I'll keep an eye on her this way.

I manage a few things and start to write up my first "Editor's Letter." Then at precisely 5:00 p.m., Harlan shows up. Suzanne gives him a frowning look. "That's *my* chair," she says to him and then turns to me. "Bye, Amy. Thanks so much for this job. I love it here!" Then she packs up Marcus and heads home for the day.

"I'm so sorry," he says, taking his hat off and wringing it in his hands.

"What happened?"

"I told you I don't drink until after noon. It was after noon."

"Harlan! You're not supposed to drink at all!"

"I know," he says quietly. "They gave me these at the shelter." He holds up a few pamphlets from Alcoholics Anonymous. "There's an AA meeting tonight at 10 p.m. I plan to go when I'm done here."

I sigh. "Can I trust you here alone?"

"Yes, ma'am," he says.

Honestly, I don't want to leave a homeless and obviously alcoholic stranger alone in my office, but I need to go somewhere to work this out. I'm still stuck on what to do with Suzanne.

Josh texted that he is working late tonight, so we won't see each other. I already miss him. He's the one I'd love to talk to about all of this.

As I walk into my apartment, my phone beeps with an incoming text. It's my brother Tad.

Congratulations! So proud of u!

I smile and text **Thnx** back. He's so sweet.

How's Josh? He texts me.

My mind turns to their conversation at my parents' yesterday.

Fine. What do you know about him that you aren't telling me?

There's a pause and then Tad texts back. **Don't want to talk about it over the phone. Let's meet.**

I, of course, want to meet *now*, but we settle on Thursday because that's the only day Tad has some free time. He says he'll pick me up at work so he can see the office. When I finally get to bed that night, it takes me a while to fall asleep. Mouser curls up beside me, and I finally drift off to her soft purrs. I dream of Suzanne growing teeth and chasing me around the office while Josh leans against my closed office door, laughing and saying people without integrity deserve what they get. When I drag myself in on Tuesday morning, there's no drunken Harlan lying on the floor, so I take this as a good sign. I wander into my office to start my day and nearly fall over with a heart attack when I open my office door.

"SURPRISE!" It's Mom and Dad, and my office is filled with balloons.

"I know you told us to give you a week to let you get settled in," Mom says in a rush, "but Josh gave us a key so we could surprise you. We got here early and will be gone before your boss comes in. We are just so proud of you, honey!" Mom wraps her arms around me and squeezes me in a hug. Dad picks up my nameplate that says *Amy Summers, Editor* on it and gives a little laugh of delight.

"I'm so proud of you," Dad says, hugging me when Mom's done.

"We'll be out of your way now," Mom says in a whisper. "Don't want to get you in trouble." Before I can even say "Thanks," they're both out the door.

"Oh," Mom turns back and hands me a key. "You can return this to Josh."

And then they're gone, leaving me in silence, surrounded by brightly colored helium balloons, one of which says "Congratulations!" on it.

I sit down at my desk. I'm wrapped up in guilt. I'm lying to everybody, but if I come clean about the lottery ticket, what will happen to my staff?

But I'm using Suzanne's money.

Then again, she slept with my boyfriend while he was still my boyfriend.

Anger suddenly passes through me. In my dream, Josh said people get what they deserve. Maybe Suzanne got what she deserved. Bart and I had dated two years. TWO years! I was so sure he was right for me. I was so sure he was going to propose. And she stole that from me.

But looking back, what did Bart and I really have in common? Maybe Suzanne did me a favor.

I'm broken out of my thoughts by my staff arriving for work. The day quickly becomes filled with meetings and planning. I don't have time to think about my problems, but every time I see Suzanne, I feel a mix of anger and guilt.

By the end of the day, I'm exhausted.

Suzanne pushes my door open. "I'm heading out." She's cradling Marcus in her arms. He looks up at his mother, gazing in such utter adoration and love. He reaches up with his tiny hand and takes hold of her hair.

"Do you need anything else before I leave?" Suzanne asks.

"Um...no," I say.

I think of Marcus growing up without a dad and without grandparents. I think of my own family and how lucky I am to have them.

"That will be all, Suzanne. Thanks."

She leaves, and I do some more paperwork that has to be done before morning. I suddenly realize it's 8 p.m. I won't see Josh tonight because he has training.

I go home to my apartment and lay out my clothes for the next day. They're nicer. I went out and bought myself some new outfits before the magazine opened. I choose a pearl blouse and some gray slacks.

Mouser hops up on the bed and begs for some attention. I play with her for a bit and feed her, but I'm too exhausted to fix myself any dinner. I have a quick bowl of cereal and go to bed. I sleep solidly and don't wake up until my alarm goes off at 6 a.m.

Chapter Thirteen

I miss Josh at work. Since I "fired" him, he has picked up another client. He's keeping busy during the day and working on his woodwork projects in between clients. We're supposed to meet for dinner, though.

Back when I was playing magazine editor as a little girl, I never realized how much work went into one issue. And how far ahead we have to plan! Magazines are usually planned months in advance, often up to six months. We only just opened in October (after a summer of planning, of course!), and we want to have our first issue out in November.

"Let's make this our 'Rethink You' issue," says my creative director. She's in her forties, very energetic, and very, well, creative. But we're careful not to make it a "better you" issue.

"I want women to realize they're good enough the way they are," I say for the umpteenth time. Everyone nods knowingly. I don't know if they agree with me because I'm the editor and boss or because they actually agree with me, but it feels good either way.

We decide to focus on style and fashion from what you already have in your closet. Pairing jeans with jackets, using scarves creatively, pulling a sweater over a dress or putting a blouse under it to get different looks, that sort of thing.

As for psychology, I contracted with a local psychologist who just happened to write a book last year called *Accepting Yourself, Accepting the Now*. This is exactly what I want for this magazine, so she's going to write an article based on that. I'll write the Editor's Corner letter, which explains what the magazine is all about and encourage women not to add anything else to their to-do list. It's almost like the opposite of self-improvement, kind of like "let's not improve" but really, that's not it at all.

"I just think when doctors tell women to go home and meditate for 40 minutes and take a yoga class twice a week, that's just adding to their stress," says the psychologist, who's in our meeting this morning. "That's just adding to their to-do list and making them feel like a failure when they can't do it. I say try three deep breaths routinely throughout the day, focus on what you're doing now, instead of all the other thoughts going through your head, and work exercise into your life. Take the stairs. Play ball with your kids. Stuff like that. The last thing busy women need is to be told that they need to do more!"

She's awesome.

So we have a great meeting, and Suzanne is there, taking notes on it all. She also brought in some bagels and some fruit. I hadn't even thought of that. She's good with touches like that I have to admit.

I work way past closing, and when I look at my watch, it's 7 p.m. I stand up, stretch, and yawn. Wow, what a day. I'm meeting Josh at 8 p.m. at the little restaurant across the street.

I finish what I'm doing and walk across a little early. I pick a table where we can see the business, the one we had on our first "date" together, which wasn't really a date. Then I see him parking his car, and I watch him walk up toward the restaurant door. He's so handsome. He's wearing a light windbreaker jacket over a black T-shirt and soft jeans. He opens the restaurant door and sees me, and his face lights up in a smile. I smile back, and my stomach does that wonderful tingly thing that it does every time I see him. I don't ever remember it doing that with Bart.

"Hi," he says and bends low to kiss me. He takes a seat, and we order sandwiches and French fries. He gets a decaf green tea.

"Coffee?" the waitress asks.

"No," I say. "Just some water."

Josh raises an eyebrow.

"I don't do caffeine after noon," I say, defensively.

But the truth is, I don't seem to need much caffeine any more. The thrill of running this magazine and the excitement of being with Josh are generating all the energy I need. I feel like I'm walking on air. Life is perfect.

Well, except for a few small things.

"Josh," I say as I'm twirling my straw in my glass, waiting for our food to come.

"Yes?"

He watches me quietly across the table. He never checks his phone while we're talking, or looks away or gets distracted by sports on TV. He's always with me when he's with me. I know that sounds weird to say it that way, but it's so cool to be the focus of someone's attention like that. When he's with me, it's as if I'm the only one in the room.

"I, uh," I'm momentarily distracted by his blue eyes. "I..." then I remember. "I want to set up a fund for Suzanne's baby, Marcus. Anonymously."

He raises his eyebrows and takes a drink of his tea. "A fund?"

"Yes," I say. "He's disabled, as you know, and his medical expenses are quite high. And I think it's terrible he is being raised without his dad or any grandparents."

I tell him what Suzanne told me about her situation.

"Will you look into it for me and see how to go about doing it?" I ask. I know Josh is great at finding out information.

"Sure," he says. "I'll see what I can find out."

Our food comes, and he tells me a little bit about his clients. He can't tell me the details (client confidentiality), but he tells me what he can. I tell him how the meeting went, and we just talk about work while we eat.

He leans back in his chair when he's finished, and I notice he's watching me as I sop up the last of my ketchup with my fry. It's funny, because with Bart, or with other men I have dated, I was always conscious of what I did or how I ate. I realize that as I've been sitting here, eating a very juicy sandwich and enjoying my fries, it never once occurred to me to be concerned with my appearance. I'm just so comfortable with Josh.

But I smile, becoming a bit uncomfortable as he keeps staring at me. "What?" I say, chewing my last fry.

He smiles that amazing smile and folds his hands behind his head. "You're just incredible," he says. "You want to set up a fund for the baby of a woman you've only known for a few weeks. Amy, your heart is just so big."

I swallow and nearly choke on my fry. "Uh, yep," I say and give a little nervous laugh.

I can't go on like this. I have to tell him.

I look into his blue eyes and know that I can trust him. "Josh..." I begin.

But then there's a loud "Hello there!" from behind me, and a large man comes over to our table and puts his hand out. Josh grabs it and they shake, the large man pumping Josh's arm heartily.

"Glen, so good to see you! How are you?" Josh says and stands. He introduces me. "This is Amy, my girlfriend."

Girlfriend. He called me his girlfriend.

"Hi, Amy," Glen grasps my hand and pumps it hard. Wow. This man has a hearty handshake. "Amy, your boyfriend here saved my life last year," he says. "I was recently divorced and had lost my job and was wandering lost in this vast world of ours." He pulls out a chair and invites himself to sit with us. "And then, this man,"—he grabs Josh's shoulder and gives it a squeeze—"helps me to figure out what I want to do with my life. Now I'm running my own boat repair shop, and I love it. I love going into work every day." He leans forward and whispers to me, "But before I met Josh, I was very near suicidal."

Then he leans back and booms a loud laugh and goes on to tell us all about his business. He talks for about 20 minutes, and I realize that it's 10 p.m.

"Josh, I've got to get home," I say. "I've gotta get some sleep!"

"Oh, I'm so sorry. I hijacked your dinner," says Glen. He really is a nice guy. Just a bit exuberant.

"That's okay. We were nearly finished," I say, and Josh stands as I do. We've already paid our bill, so we walk to the door together. After Glen leaves and Josh has walked me to my car, I say to him, "You're so amazing. I like that you help so many people."

"You should have seen Glen when he first came to me," Josh says. "He was thin, his face was gray, and there was no light in his eyes. He looked so sad."

"He's anything but that now, it seems," I say.

Josh puts his hands on my shoulders and then tenderly brushes a lock of my hair behind my ear. "You're beautiful," he says quietly.

"So are you," I say. He leans forward, and we kiss. It's like floating on air. It's so amazing to be in love with your best friend.

In love? Is that what I am?

After we kiss, he stands there, still looking at me. "It's late," he says. And it is. I have no idea how I'll get up in the morning.

"I know..." I want more. He leans in, kisses me again, and then puts his arms around me. He's warm and smells so good. I never want this to end.

But it does. "You need some sleep," he says. "We'll have more time together over the weekend." And he opens my car door for me, always the gentleman.

I climb in.

"Oh, was there something you were about to tell me before Glen came in?" Josh asks.

Oh, that. I remember now. I was about to tell him about the lottery ticket and who Suzanne really is and why I have all this guilt about her baby not having enough money.

But I don't want to ruin the moment, I'm tired, and that's going to be a long conversation.

"No. It can wait," I say.

So we say good night. He closes my door, and I drive off. I glance back in my rearview mirror, and he's still standing there, his hands in his pockets, watching me until I'm gone.

Chapter Fourteen

On Thursday, Tad cancels lunch. Charlie had hives, and they had to take him to the ER. It turns out that he is okay, but now Tad doesn't have time to meet with me.

Suzanne asks if she can order me some lunch.

"That sounds great," I say. We decide on a sub sandwich shop that delivers. While we're waiting, Suzanne comes back into my office.

"Amy, do you have a minute? I want to show you something."

I invite her in. She sits down across from my desk and spreads some papers across its surface, so I can see them.

"As I was filing, I saw these, and I came up with a few ideas," she says. They are photocopies of the expense reports detailing our costs across the board for maintenance, supplies, running the presses, etc. They're marked up with red pen.

"I found a maintenance company that's cheaper, and they seem better. They offer regular maintenance work, like we can set up once-a-month standing appointments, and they have a 24-hour call line." Her hand travels down the paper to the last column. "You can see here that the annual cost is cheaper, and yet we get more hours of service from them."

Which is true.

"Then here," says Suzanne. "I found that our paper costs are really high. If we buy from this company," she points to a scribbled name on the margin, "we can cut our costs almost by a third. We have to buy in bulk, which means our upfront costs are more and there's the problem of storage, but I found a room on the third floor where we can store the paper. Overall, it saves us this much annually." She points to another figure.

"Wow," I say. She's pretty amazing. She has saved me quite a bit of money with just those two changes. "That's... that's awesome."

"Do you want me to call the companies tomorrow and make the changes?" she asks.

"Um, yes. That would be great. Thank you, Suzanne."

She leaves, and I sit there for a few minutes, trying to sort out my feelings for her. Just before closing time, I get a call from the local newspaper wanting to interview me. I talk to them for a bit and then send the call to Suzanne to fit into my calendar.

I so love having a personal assistant. If only she hadn't slept with my ex...

It turns out I've become a Big Deal in town. Everybody wants to talk to me before the first issue comes out. Over the next two weeks, Suzanne sets up a ton of interviews, and I am invited to luncheons, including the local Women's Business luncheon. I invite Josh as my date.

He shows up wearing a navy suit with a silky gray shirt under it. He looks so handsome in a suit! The luncheon goes well, but I hardly have time to talk to Josh because all of the woman are coming up and talking to me. I give out the number of our advertising person to several, like the local cake decorator, a woman who's a naturopath physician, and a photographer. They all want to advertise with us.

This goes on for days. Luncheons, dinners, interviews. I'm running out of things to wear.

Josh drops me off at my apartment late one evening after dinner with the Downtown Development Chairperson. I'm exhausted and my feet are killing me from my heels, but I don't want Josh to go.

"We hardly get to talk anymore," I say. I've been missing the easy days over the summer, when we spent so much time together.

"I know," he says, kissing me. He looks at me, his fingers playing lightly with my hair. "I miss you."

It's a funny thing to say because we are together so much, but I know exactly what he means.

"Do you want to come up?"

"Yes," he says.

But we both know it's too late for that. It's nearly midnight. Reluctantly, I let him go and open the door to my apartment complex with my key.

We kiss one last time, and then I go up. He always waits until I'm safely inside before he leaves, so I turn my light on, go stand by the window, and wave at him.

The next day, Suzanne knocks on my office door.

"Do you have a minute?" she asks.

"Sure. Come in."

She sits down, and I can tell she has something she wants to say.

"I love it here," she says. "And I know you worry about Marcus, so I wanted you to know that someone is giving him money. There's been a trust fund set up to cover his health care costs and provide money for special education."

So Josh got it set up. I settle back in my chair.

"It's helping so much. I just thought you would want to know."

"That's awesome," I say. "I'm glad Marcus is okay."

We're quiet for a minute, and then I think I should ask, "Do you know who set it up?"

"No. It's anonymous. But I think it's my ex. I think he finally felt guilty but didn't want to get involved. You know. Maybe he's coming around. Do you think? I think he's a jerk, but Marcus could use a daddy."

Her *ex*? She thinks her ex–*my* ex–set this up?

I'm not sure what to say. Anger boils up in me, and I instantly regret that I did what I did. I don't like Bart getting the credit. But it's helping Marcus, not her, I remind myself.

"So I wanted to ask you if I could have some vacation time around Christmas?" Suzanne says. "I know I haven't accumulated any yet, but I can afford to take some time off now, and my sister has invited me out to visit her."

A word comes to mind that rhymes with witch.

"Amy? Is something wrong? If December isn't a good time..."

"No, it's fine," I say, recovering. "It's fine. Write out what days you want off and let me know. We'll work something out. Harlan has mentioned he has some phone and office skills."

Suzanne has come around about Harlan. They hardly ever see each other, but when they do, they get along. It helps that Harlan has quit drinking.

Which reminds me: Harlan has invited me to an AA meeting. He says it's an open meeting, and they're giving out medals or something. He is thirty days sober and wants me to come.

After Suzanne leaves for the day, I pack up my things and look at the time. Harlan's meeting is in twenty minutes, so I have time to walk because it's only four blocks away. I amble down the street, taking my time and window-shopping a little bit. There's a really nice shirt in one of the windows that I think Josh would look great in. It's a heather blue Henley. It has short sleeves, so it would show off his arms.

Which are nicely muscled.

I find the right address for the meeting. It's in the basement of a building that serves as a coffee shop, a karate studio, and a deli. All on different floors. The basement looks as if it's overflow space for the karate studio, because it's a big room, almost like a gym, with a circle of chairs in it. There're some people milling around, and somebody is setting out Styrofoam cups for coffee. I get a cup and look around for Harlan.

"Amy!" he says, and I see him coming down the stairs. "I'm so glad you could make it."

We give each other a brief hug, which seems awkward, and then Harlan says, "I see you found the coffee," because there's not much else to say.

Someone asks people to sit, so we all take a chair in the circle. It's nearly full and there are adults of all ages here, both men and women. There's a woman sitting across from me with a business suit on who seems ill at ease.

A man who I assume must be a leader welcomes everybody, and we all go around and say our names. When it comes to me, I say "I'm Amy, a friend of Harlan's" and everybody says "Hi, Amy."

"Aren't you that woman who is starting up that magazine?" says a voice from across the circle. It's the nervous woman in the business suit.

"Uh...yes." I say.

"You think we're good enough the way we are? I think that's a bunch of crap."

I'm startled for a moment. Who is this woman anyway?

"Charlotte, it's good you're sharing your feelings," says the man who I think is the leader. "But she is only visiting with us today. Let's not attack her."

"Her magazine is called *Good Enough*," the woman continues. "Honey, I drank myself into a stupor every night for six years, lost my husband and lost my kids. Do you think I'm good enough the way I am?"

"But you are sober now, Charlotte," the leader-man says.

"Am I? Because I might not be drinking, but am I really sober?" she counters. "What does sober mean, anyway?"

She throws a challenging look around the room.

"You own a magazine?" somebody else says. I think her name is Hannah.

"I'm the editor, actually," I say.

"Define 'Good Enough,'" says Charlotte. She's really not going to let this go.

"Uh…well, we are all created with…" I'm struggling for words. I'm a writer, and here I am struggling for words because this woman's anger has thrown me off. Everyone is looking at me.

"Amy's good enough the way she is," says a man, who I believe said his name was Eric. I really should have paid more attention. "She's here trying to get sober just like the rest of us. I don't think you should downplay her struggles just because she owns a magazine. She's trying, just like we all are."

I want to tell them that I am just visiting, not in recovery, but some of them are looking daggers at me now. I swallow hard. Harlan glances over at me.

"Amy doesn't drink," he says.

"How can we trust what that magazine prints now anyway?" says Hannah, who obviously wasn't listening to Harlan.

"She no longer drinks, as Eric said. She's in recovery," says the leader-man.

"Actually…" I begin.

"Honey, I think it's fabulous that you are here," says another woman. "Don't let Charlotte mess with you. She's just having a hard time and tends to take it out on others," This woman gives Charlotte a look and then turns back to me. "Welcome to the group, Amy. When was the last time you drank?"

"It was…" I'm not sure what to say. Then I remember the bottle of champagne I drowned my troubles with in my apartment.

"April," I say.

"April?" There's a murmur of astonishment around the room. "So more than six months of sobriety! Congratulations!"

The leader-man beams at me. "Do you care to share how you've made it this long?" he asks.

"No, you don't understand," I say, a bit desperately. "I don't have a problem with alcohol."

The room falls quiet. Then I hear Charlotte's voice. "Denial." She snorts and crosses her arms.

Harlan clears his throat and stands up. "Amy is here as a guest of mine," he says. "She is not an alcoholic."

There's a moment of quiet. Even Charlotte looks a little crestfallen.

"That's right," I say. "I'm just here with Harlan." Then I learn towards Harlan and whisper, "Thank you."

The leader-man clears his throat. "Well, Amy, good to have you join us. Now that we have that cleared up, let's get started. Let me introduce today's speaker."

A woman walks to the front of the room and shares an incredible story for about 45 minutes. It's heart breaking, and I find myself wiping tears away more than once. Finally, they ask if anybody is having an anniversary.

"I am." Harlan holds his hand up sheepishly. "It's thirty days for me today."

People say congratulations and many of them clap. The leader-man pulls out a medal that resembles a round coin and hands it to Harlan. Harlan's eyes grow a little misty as he fingers it.

"Thank you," he says. "And I'd especially like to thank Amy. When she first met me, I was a mess. But she believed in me and gave me a chance. I wouldn't be here without her."

I wasn't expecting that, and tears come to my eyes again. Then the leader-man adjourns the meeting.

The next day is crazy busy again. I have no idea how people manage to run magazines. I'm having enough trouble just remembering who all of my staff are.

I'm sitting at my desk, dawdling over my first Editor's Corner letter, which is due very soon. It's going to run in the November issue, our first issue. I'm so thankful to be where I am, and I wonder if it's too cliché to focus on "thanks" for the November issue.

I'm thankful for…Josh comes to mind first. Of all the things that have happened to me this year—the lottery ticket, the magazine—none of them compares to Josh. He has made me feel alive and loved and…well, good enough. When I'm with him, I feel amazing, and I think about him all the time. His blue eyes, the way his jeans fit him so comfortably, his…

"Amy?"

It's Suzanne, sticking her head in. "Your 1:00 is here."

Oh. I forgot about that. I quickly close my laptop and nod to her. "Send him in."

He, meaning the director of Girls Town, the local facility for troubled teens. These kids are incarcerated for anything from theft to murder, but all of them have come from very bad backgrounds. It's almost like they didn't have a chance from the start.

Thomas Deker, the director, enters and shakes my hand. "Amy," he says warmly. "Nice to meet you in person."

We've talked on the phone twice. He seems every bit as warm as his voice sounds, and yet there's a strength in his tall, thin frame that I wouldn't want to mess with.

"So what do you think?"

He called me last week to see if I would consider publishing a series of essays from his girls, maybe in the spring issues. They'd be about life choices and about what the girls want to do once they "make it" out of Girls Town. They'd also be about how they got in there. Gritty stuff. Powerful stuff.

"I think it's a great idea," I say. And I do. Imagine if women reading these essays wanted to help these girls!

"Suppose a business owner decides to mentor a girl who wants to open a restaurant?" I say. "Or suppose a teacher mentors a girl who wants to work with kids?"

Part of the series would be for us to look for mentors. I get so excited thinking about it.

Thomas and I talk for quite a while. After he leaves, I realize that I have my Editor's Corner letter figured out. I sit down and write for a full two hours, until everyone has left for the day. When I finish, I reread it. It's about how thankful I am for the opportunities I have in my life, my good parents, my education, and now my dream job. But it's also about taking where we're at and doing the best with that because we can. Because we are uniquely and wonderfully made.

It's late when I finish, and I pick up my phone to call Josh.

"Dinner?" he says as soon as he picks up.

"Dinner!" I say. I'm starved.

Josh meets me at my apartment with some Chinese takeout. He smiles when he sees me pull up. His whole face lights up when I walk toward him. I feel my stomach churning with butterflies again. Every time I see him, it's like waking up from a great dream and realizing it's a day off work, so you can snuggle down in the covers and go back to sleep to dream some more. He's that comforting, that good, that snuggly to be near.

"Amy," he says and kisses me. My heart quickens, and for a moment, nothing else exists. Then he reaches past me and opens the door to my apartment with my keys. I open my eyes, and we walk upstairs together.

Unfortunately, Mrs. Crabbs is out in the hall. She raises her eyebrows as she sucks on her cigarette, but doesn't say anything.

I smile sweetly at her and let Josh open my apartment door.

"Shacking up?" she calls out as we enter. I close the door and Josh and I both laugh. I realize I've turned red. I quickly go into the kitchen for plates before he sees.

Josh asks if I have any matches, and I hand him some. He lights the candle I have on my table as I set plates out. Then he wanders over to my stereo and puts in a CD that he brought. It's a beautiful instrumental with strings. Maybe a dulcimer and some Spanish guitar.

"Nice," I say. I wasn't expecting all of this.

"It's been a while since we had any time together," he says. "I thought it would be nice to have a bit of romance."

He pulls out my chair, and when I sit, my shoulder brushes his hand. I'm suddenly aware of my hair and wonder if I look okay after my long day at work. But Josh reaches down from behind me and kisses me softly on the back of my neck. "I missed you," he says softly.

I close my eyes, drinking in his closeness. Then he's gone and sitting down across from me. He has ordered my favorites, almond chicken and lo mein. He always remembers what I like.

"I feel like we should have wine or something," I say, "but I don't have any alcohol in my apartment."

"We don't need wine," he says. "Water is fine."

He holds up his glass. "To Amy and her first editor's letter." We clink them together.

Dinner is nice, and we talk about work, his new client, and my letter from the editor. Afterwards, he helps me clean up.

I don't have a dishwasher, so Josh takes washing duty while I dry. I can't help but notice his biceps bulging as he scrubs off our plates. He glances at me, and I look away, pretending to be busy with drying the glass I'm holding. Mouser winds between my legs, looking for attention.

Afterwards, he wipes up the counter and then goes back to the table.

"Fortune cookie?" he asks, holding one up.

"Sure," I say. We take them to the couch and sit side by side.

"You first," I say. He breaks his cookie in two and pulls out the little piece of paper.

"'The fortune you seek is in another cookie.' What?" he laughs. "I got ripped off."

"That just means you get to eat another cookie," I say.

"Open yours," he says eagerly, like a little kid.

I do. "'A kiss can beautify souls, hearts, and lives,'" I read. Our eyes meet.

"It's not that you need anything to beautify you even more," he says, taking my hand and tracing the back of it with his fingers. I close my eyes at the warmth of his touch and his fingers travel to my wrist. "You're already beautiful, Amy." He caresses my cheek with the back of his hand, and I look at him. I look at those wonderful, warm, blue eyes of his that make me feel so good. My breathing quickens, and I press my cheek against his hand. It travels down to my neck and then against my back as he gently pulls me toward him. I take his free hand in mine and lean in to the kiss.

Whenever Josh touches me, I feel like I've come home. Like a part of me that has forever been missing is finally there. His kiss just makes it that much more obvious that we belong together.

I feel his steamy breath on my face. My heart is pounding, and I am lost in his kiss. It seems like there is nothing else in the room. Just Josh and me. His mouth travels to my ear, and his breathing is fast. We stay that way for a few moments, together, touching, his fingers trailing through my hair.

"Amy, I love you," he whispers. It's the first time he has used those words. Something inside of me melts, and I know now, more than ever, that the feeling I had the first time I saw him was this. Love. Only now, after so many months of friendship, I can truly say he's my best friend and so much more.

"I love you too," I say, and I mean it. He pulls me harder against him, and we kiss there on my couch with Mouser making feeble attempts to get in between us.

But nothing is going to get between us. In Josh's arms, I am where I'm supposed to be.

Chapter Fifteen

November comes fast, and our first issue is out. We celebrate with a huge catered luncheon for everybody, and I invite my parents. There's a ton of food, and I circulate for a while, talking to everybody, before I sit down with a plate of food at the table with my parents and Josh. It's very informal–we're just in the cafeteria–but I wanted to do something to celebrate with the staff.

Somebody opens a bottle of champagne, but I pass. I've never really been a drinker.

"Amy," Mom leans over to whisper conspiratorially in my ear. "Janet saw you coming out of an AA meeting the other day. Is there something you want to tell me?"

Janet is my parents' next-door neighbor. She's known for gossip.

"Mom, I was there with Harlan."

"Who?"

That's right. Mom doesn't know about Harlan. It is hard to remember what I haven't told my family.

"It's okay," Mom pats me on the shoulder. "Your dad and I support you. We're here to help."

"Mom…"

"I knew something was up when you had that mini break-down back when Bart dumped you."

I glance at Josh, but he's talking to our advertiser.

"If you need us to help…" Mom winks and quits talking because Josh is looking at me.

"Mom, I'm not an alcoholic," I say.

"Honey, isn't the first step to admit —" But she is interrupted as Andrea arrives and sits next to me.

"Amy! SO sorry I'm late. Traffic jam on Jackson Road. Oh, there's food." She immediately jumps up and heads toward the buffet.

I smile at Josh, and we manage to get through lunch without talking about anything upsetting, like my ex or me owning this magazine. Or my "alcoholism." I'll have to talk to Mom later and straighten this out.

When everybody is about finished eating, I stand up and move up to the front of the room. I clear my throat.

Everyone looks up, expectantly.

"This magazine is a huge success already," I say. "It's due to all of you who are here."

I give a short talk as the Editor, thanking everyone who has made this successful. I look at my parents.

"And to Mom and Dad. Thank you for being here, and thank you for always believing in me. It's because of you that I've had the time and opportunities that have led me here."

Mom wipes a tear from her eyes, and I think Dad gets a bit weepy too.

Then I look at Josh.

"And I wouldn't be here at all without Josh Gray," I say. He smiles at me in that way that he has. His eyes crinkle a little, and I can tell he loves me just by the way he looks at me.

"Josh was my inspiration. I was at a crossroads in my life, unsure of where to go next. Josh helped get me on that path that led me here. He reminded me that I was good enough to do this. Good enough."

Everybody claps, and then things wind down and people start to leave to get back to work. We're all hugging and congratulating each other.

"Where's the owner?" somebody asks. I turn. It's Carl from the mailroom. Everyone here thinks I'm just the editor. "We never see the owner."

"He wants to remain anonymous," I say.

"I'd love to meet him," says Carl. "What's he like?"

Josh has been briefed on this. He has known all along I want to remain anonymous as the owner. "I'm sure that he—or she—is very generous," says Josh.

People nod and the lunchroom clears out, except for my parents and Josh.

"We're so proud of you, Amy," Mom says and hugs me. Then Josh has to get back to work, and I am left alone, in my cafeteria, in my building, with food that I paid for.

I can't believe how much my life has changed in six months.

Suzanne runs into my office, out of breath.

"Amy!" she gasps, whispering. "I have MYRA WINN-REY'S booking agent on the phone for you!!"

"What?"

"MYRA WINNREY!" Suzanne squeals. "Her booking agent. For YOU."

Oh my gosh. I ask Suzanne to transfer the call into my office, and when it rings, I pick up the receiver with trembling hands.

"Hello? Amy Summers," I say, trying to keep my voice from shaking.

Myra Winnrey is huge. HUGE. If you make it on her show, you've made it. She is interested in all things geared toward helping people. Toward making you a better you. Or me a better me.

Oh my gosh. I can't believe they are calling ME.

A man's voice answers. In a business-like manner, he tells me that Myra wants me on her show. Before I know it, we've set up a plan for me to fly out to New York next Thursday and appear on her show live that very day. It airs at 4 p.m. I'll get a 15-minute segment, and then they will fly me back home.

"What does she want to talk about?" I ask.

"About being Good Enough. About what inspired you to start up this magazine. You don't need to prepare anything. Just answer her questions and let Myra lead. You'll be fine."

When he hangs up, I'm still trembling. I quickly grab my phone and call Josh.

"Really?" he says when I tell him. He sounds so excited for me. "That's awesome! Do you want me to come with you?"

Of course, I want him to come with me! Oh my gosh. Josh and me in New York City with MYRA WINNREY!

I don't think I'll ever be able to sleep again.

What will I wear?

After I talk to Josh, I call Andrea.

"OH MY GOSH!" Her squeal can be heard for miles, I'm sure.

"But what do I wear?" I say.

"Girlfriend, we're going shopping after work today," she says.

After five stores, Andrea and I agree on a gray pencil skirt and salmon silk blouse with a striking turquoise scarf. Andrea helps me find just the right jewelry to go with it. "And Spanx," she says. She eyes my rear end. "You look pretty good, but we can all use a little help."

So I grab the Spanx as well, to hold all my jiggly parts together underneath it all.

The next few days are crazy, and I'm a bundle of nerves, waiting for next week to come. But Tad calls me up Friday and asks if he can take me to lunch. My stomach lurches as I remember that he was going to tell me what he knows about Josh.

I agree to meet him at a café a few streets over, at noon.

Tad is already there when I arrive. He is sitting there squeezing some lemon into his hot tea. He looks up and smiles at me, his brown eyes sparkling.

"Sis," he says and motions for me to sit. "I ordered you a tea."

"Thanks," I say, and am taking my coat off when it arrives. It's green tea, my favorite. I put a pack of sugar and a bit of lemon in it and stir, waiting for Tad to say something first. I'm not sure I want to know what he knows. Things are so perfect with Josh. I can't imagine what Tad could say that would change how I feel about Josh. Yet my stomach is doing flip-flops.

We order sandwiches, and while we're waiting, Tad clears his throat and looks across the table at me.

"So you want to know how I know Josh," he says.

109

"Well...yes. You told me to be careful, that 'it's all probably fine.' What does that mean?"

"And it all probably is fine," says Tad. He sighs and sits back in his chair.

"Remember when I was up for a construction award a few years back for my work on the library's new reading room?" I nod. The reading room is beautiful. Tad designed it, and his company built it. It has this huge atrium in it with skylights. It is lit with natural light from the windows and is a wonderful place to sit and read, especially on a sunny day.

"Well, at the awards banquet, which you didn't attend because you were off on that mother/daughter trip with Mom..."

Oh yeah, that. Mom was so excited that she had tickets to a Neil Diamond concert. She invited me to it (mostly so I'd drive, I'm sure), and then we spent the night at this fancy hotel nearby and had pedicures the next day. It was fun.

"So anyway, at the awards banquet, Josh and I were up for the same award. He was up for a project he worked on over on the west side. When they announced him as the winner, he got up to give his talk and something changed in his face. He was all lit up, and then his face just sort of crumpled. He said that he couldn't accept the award and graciously thanked everyone. He sat back down, ordered a drink, and downed it. Then left the banquet early."

I wasn't sure where this story was going.

"Anyway, the votes had already been tabulated, and they couldn't give the award to anyone else. But the fact is, Amy, that I would have probably gotten that award if it wasn't given to Josh. That would have done huge things for my career and my company. But he got it. He deserved it because the work he did was fabulous, but he just threw it away."

I see. So Tad is upset with Josh because of that.

"So you're upset with him because you lost to him?" I ask.

Tad scowls. "No. I'm not upset with him. He was going through a hard time then. His friend had just been killed on site, and he witnessed it. But what I wanted you to know was that I heard that Josh began drinking after that night. He also did a string of drugs and wound up getting arrested for marijuana possession."

I'm dumbfounded. Drug use? Josh? I think about his clear, blue eyes, his certainty, and his calm demeanor. I can't imagine him being upset enough about anything to use drugs. He doesn't even drink caffeine!

"No," I say.

"Amy, it's not up for debate. It happened. He lost his builder's license and his job because he showed up high at work. But he seems fine now. I just wanted you to know."

I sit there for a while, too stunned to speak.

"So I take it he never told you."

I shake my head. Then I think of Bart and all the things he never told me either.

Before I know it, a tear is escaping the corner of my eye.

"Amy..." Tad says. Our sandwiches arrive, and I dab my eye with my napkin.

"It's okay," I say after the waitress leaves.

"I'm sure he's fine now. It was a few years ago. I just wanted you to know because you seem really taken with him, and I don't want him to...well...relapse on you."

I nod. "Thanks for telling me," I manage to choke out.

It's not that I'm upset about him being a former drug user. It's that he didn't tell me. For as long as we've been together, it should have been something he shared. But then come to think of it, I don't know much about his family or anything. We always talk about me and my work. Me. Then the guilt hits me because I clearly have not been telling Josh everything either. I'm just as bad.

"Amy?" Tad says gently. I look up. "I thought you knew. I thought maybe that's where you met him. At AA."

"What?"

"Alcoholics Anonymous. Mom says you've been going to AA meetings. She says you got so desperate you even drank the bottle of wine from my wedding. The souvenir one that you were supposed to age until your own wedding."

"Oh my gosh. I'm not an alcoholic." I tell Tad what really happened.

He laughs long and hard. "Oh, Amy. I knew that wasn't you. I told Mom and Dad you hated the taste of alcohol. You were such a good girl in school. We just thought maybe Bart had driven you over the edge."

We laugh together, but I can't get my mind off Josh. I don't remember much of what else Tad and I talk about while we finish our sandwiches, but by the time I get back to work, I have a headache. I spend the afternoon alone in my office, pondering what Tad had told me.

Chapter Sixteen

"The first issue was a huge success!" Josh says when he calls me that evening. "HUGE." He reads off the numbers in sales, and they're good. Really good.

But I can't get too excited because I keep thinking about what Tad told me.

"Josh, can we get together to talk this evening?" I say.

"Over Chinese or Italian?" he says.

I don't answer.

"Uh-oh. It's never good news when the girl says 'we have to talk,'" says Josh.

"Let's meet at that little Italian restaurant on Fifth," I say. "Seven o'clock."

"Okay. Amy, is everything all right?"

"I hope so."

I get there early and pick a private booth at the back of the restaurant. When Josh arrives, I've torn my napkin into tiny shreds and quickly try to hide them.

"Nervous?" Josh says as he sits down across from me, his blue eyes troubled.

"Josh..."

The waitress comes and brings us water. We both order tea—he gets decaf—and then she leaves again.

"What happened three years ago at the construction awards banquet?" There. I started it.

Josh sits back, clearly not expecting this topic of conversation.

"I was given an award, and I refused it," he says.

"Why?"

He takes a deep breath and laces his fingers together. "Because it should have been Scott up there getting that award. The project was his idea, his creation. I just got it because I was part of his team. We worked together, but the truth is it was more him. I wasn't much without him. So I couldn't accept it. The..." he swallows. "The pain was just still too fresh."

He laces and unlaces his fingers. "I know your brother was up for it too. I recognized him right away when I was at your parents' house for dinner. I suspect he would have won it if I hadn't. His library project was fantastic. But I won it, and I threw it away. Is that how you found out? Tad?"

I nod.

"Is there anything else you want to tell me?" I ask, my voice a little shaky.

Josh swallows and then shakes his head.

The waitress comes to take our orders. "Nothing yet," I say. "Just tea for now." She leaves. Josh glances up at me.

"Were you on drugs?" I ask. There. I just blurted it out.

Josh's eyes widen and then flash with anger. "Who told you that?"

"Tad."

"How did he...?"

I don't like the anger I see in Josh's eyes. I've never seen him angry before. But he takes a deep breath and continues, his voice low. "Yes, Amy, I was on drugs. After that night, I started drinking, because every time I closed my eyes I saw that beam falling on Scott. For a while, the drinking helped me to sleep, but then even that wasn't enough. I was at a bar one evening with the guys from work, and somebody offered me some pot. We went back to his place, and I got high for the first time. It wasn't like you think, in a slum, in an alley. This guy had a nice house, a flat screen TV, and all the amenities. We were watching a football game on TV when it happened. All I know is the pain went away for the first time since the accident. So I started using it regularly. I went in to work high one day and got fired. Shortly after that, I checked myself into rehab. I knew I was headed downhill, that I needed help, and that Scott would not have wanted me to feel this way. The accident wasn't my fault, but you see, I was there, so it seemed like I could have stopped it somehow."

He looks across the table at me, and the anger is gone. His eyes are filled with pain, and he looks so vulnerable. I swallow.

"Why didn't you tell me?" I ask, quietly.

He shrugs. "I don't know. Because it's no longer an issue. Because I'm a different person now. Because I was afraid I'd lose you."

I think about all the things Bart kept from me. The lies and the secrets when I thought everything was real. When I thought he was this amazing person who went off to Haiti to help people and he was really in the next town doing his secretary.

"Have I?" Josh asks.

"Have you what?"

"Lost you?"

Tears fill my eyes, and I get up and go around the table. I put my arms around his shoulders and whisper into his ear. "No. You haven't lost me." And I hug him. Because this is different. From the start, Josh and I have had a different relationship than Bart and I had. Josh loves me for who I am. He has never asked me to be more. And the way he looks at me—Bart never looked at me like that. Only Josh doesn't know the real me. It's time to tell him.

Just then, my cell phone rings. I ignore it, but the person hangs up and rings again. And then texts. I go back to my seat and pull it out of my purse.

"It's a text from Suzanne," I say, "She says to call her ASAP."

So I do.

"Amy! I gave Myra Winnrey's agent my number, and he called me at home. Myra wants to talk to you, so I gave her your number. She'll be calling any minute."

Just then, another call beeps in. It's a number I don't know, from New York City.

"Oh my gosh, it's her!" I say.

"Well take it!" Suzanne says and hangs up.

"Myra Winnrey," I mouth to Josh as I answer the phone.

"Hello? This is Amy Summers..."

"Amy! Myra Winnrey here!"

"Hello, Ms. Winnrey," I say. I notice my voice is shaking.

"I'm looking forward to talking with you next Thursday! I just wanted to say to show up with what you want to wear on my show and bring the December copy of your magazine so you can show it off nationally. It'll be a blast."

"Wow. Okay. I'm looking forward to it!"

"Tally-ho," she says and hangs up. Myra isn't English, but she always says "Tally-ho" at the end of her show and gives a little wave.

The phone call only took about 30 seconds, but the mood at the table has changed. I'm shaking from excitement, for one thing.

"Wow," I say again and look over at Josh.

"Myra?" he says. "That's something, Amy. You've really come a long way."

I look across the table at him and stretch my hands out. He takes them in his warm, strong ones. "I wouldn't be here without you, Josh," I say.

"Amy, I'm sorry. I should have told you. I know you've been hurt before, and I should have been truthful right from the start."

"Oh, Josh, it's okay," I say. He squeezes my hands.

"I'm always going on about honesty and integrity with my clients. I guess I could use a lesson in that myself," he says. "I never lied to you, but I never told you either. We shouldn't have secrets."

Oh. Suddenly, with a great weight of shame, my own secret comes back to mind. I need to tell Josh about the lottery ticket and where my money is really from. I need to now, because I did lie to him.

A text beeps in. I ignore it and continue looking at Josh.

"Josh…" I begin.

Then I get another text. And then a third.

Josh laughs. "You'd better look at that."

"It's Suzanne again," I say, glancing down at my phone. I call her back and tell her what Myra said. Then Mom texts me with a photo of Dad in a new cap he bought.

"Call your mom," Josh says. "Tell her. It's exciting!"

So I do. Then our dinner arrives, and Josh is excitedly talking about Myra while I am texting Suzanne. She is making my final flight plans. The evening gets crazy and Josh and I don't get to talk any more.

I'll tell him after the Myra show, I promise myself. We'll have a proper sit-down discussion, and I'll tell him. And then I'll tell my parents. And I need to come clean with Suzanne as well.

Despite all of the excitement of the day, I sleep well that night because I'm so exhausted.

Chapter Seventeen

With Christmas just next month, Josh is selling a lot of his woodwork. He sold a carved wooden bed frame to a newlywed couple. He sold a table and set of chairs, a few spice racks and a rocking chair. He even sold some house plans. They weren't a Christmas present for someone but he was excited about designing them.

I love to watch him work. On Wednesday night, I go over to his house for dinner because he's busy finishing the house plans. I sit on the sofa and watch him at his drafting table (which he made, by the way, and it's really awesome). Besides, it takes my mind off the fact that we're leaving tomorrow for New York City.

He's bent over his drafting table, quiet, his strong hands folding out his blueprints and carefully smoothing out the creases. Then he takes up his pencil and starts to sketch.

His hands work in a rhythmic movement, and the only sound is his pencil on paper, the soft "scritch-scritch" of his work. He is so lost in his work that he's barely aware that I'm in the room. I get to see another side of him while he is doing what it is he was made to do, a private side that I rarely see.

Finally, I get up, which startles him, and rummage through his fridge for dinner. Josh's fridge, like the rest of his life, is so well ordered. I find some green peppers and an onion.

"Spaghetti?" I ask.

"Sounds good."

I start chopping vegetables on the wooden chopping block that he made. It's relaxing, my chopping and his steady "scritch-scitch." I start to imagine how it would be if every night was like this, and I lived here.

When the spaghetti is done, he leaves the drafting table, although he has some work to finish up later tonight. We have a relaxing dinner, and because tomorrow is a big day for me too, I go home early.

A copy of the December issue is sitting on my bag, which I packed early with the help of Andrea. She knows just how to pack clothes without wrinkling them. But I did take a travel iron just in case.

The December issue hasn't been released yet, but the cover is spectacular. Our photographer captured a woman sitting on a chair with a mess in the background. She's holding her three-year-old daughter on her lap. Her face is against the child's cheek, and there's an unmistakable look of joy on both their faces. The photographer captured them perfectly and softened the background edges of the messy room they are in. A caption on the cover reads "The Simple Joys of Living." The article is about setting limits on work hours. Work of all types, be it in the office or at home.

After I recheck my packing thrice to be sure I've got everything, I go to bed. Mouser curls up at my feet, and I fall asleep to the sound of her rhythmic purring.

Josh picks me up at 9 a.m. I am so nervous I want to throw up.

After a warm embrace and a kiss, he says, "Ready?"

"Yes," I swallow.

He drives us to the airport, and we park the car and get on our plane. As the plane takes off for New York City, he reaches over and takes my hand.

"I'm excited for you," he says.

I nod. I'm beyond words at the moment. In six hours, I'll be sitting on Myra's couch in front of a gazillion television viewers showing off the cover of my new magazine. My heart quickens for a minute—did I forget it?—but I pat my laptop case and no, the cover is there inside. I'm just a nervous wreck.

Josh leans over and gives me a little kiss on the cheek. I turn and meet his lips. "You'll do fine," he says. "And if it's not perfect, that's kind of the point of your magazine, right?"

He's so right. I sigh and lean my head on his shoulder. I didn't sleep well last night, and I'm so tired. With the hum of the plane engines and Josh's comforting warmth underneath my head, I'm soon sound asleep.

In no time, he's whispering, "Time to wake up," and my ears are popping as the plane descends. There it is below us—

New York City. I see the Statue of Liberty and Ellis Island. Then the plane circles and descends some more, and in no time, it seems, we are in Manhattan.

"Look!" I gasp. As we get off the plane, I see a man in a tux standing there holding a sign that says "Amy Summers." That's our driver. We have our very own *driver*!

It's not far to Myra's studio, but apparently, in New York, they measure driving in time instead of miles. With the traffic, it takes us a while to get where we're going. There's so much to see out the windows, and I keep pointing things out to Josh. There are stores I'd love to shop in and restaurants I'd love to eat in. I see a famous talk show host's television studio and the place where they used to make soap operas.

Then there it is. Myra Winnrey's studio.

My stomach lurches again, and Josh squeezes my hand. He has barely let go of it since we left the airport back in Michigan.

"You'll do fine," he says.

Our driver lets us off at the back door, where yellow tape and bodyguards are keeping the crowd back. As I walk toward the back door, people cheer and wave at me, although I'm pretty sure none of them know who I am. But I'm going into Myra Winnrey's studio, so they must figure I'm somebody.

I'm going into Myra Winnrey's studio!

Oh my gosh. I think I might die.

"You'll be fine," Josh whispers. I think he can read my mind.

We're met at the door by a very nice and busy-looking young man who ushers us in and closes the door.

"Welcome," he says, pumping our hands. "This way."

He leads us down the hall into a room with a table covered with trays of sandwiches, pickles, cheese, fruits and an assortment of small muffins.

"Lunch," he says. "Take your time and eat. I'll be back in 30 minutes to take you to makeup."

Josh and I look at each other. There's all this food and nobody else in the room.

"Wow," I say. I don't think I can eat. I'm too nervous.

Josh, on the other hands, shrugs and grabs a muffin. He stuffs the whole thing in his mouth (it's tiny) and mumbles, "Dry."

Then he takes a plate and loads on a sandwich and some other stuff. He tosses me a pear. "Eat," he says.

I look at the pear and take a small bite. That ignites my appetite, and I decide to have a turkey sandwich and get some protein in me.

"This is amazing," I say, chewing and looking around the room. "I can't believe we're here."

Josh gives me his smile and says, "I can. You're amazing, Amy. You can do anything you set your mind to."

We finish lunch and some woman comes in. She's severe looking with her hair in a ponytail that is too tight.

She glances at us and then takes a second glance at Josh. "You," she points at him with a pen. "Who are you?"

"Um…he's my boyfriend." I say before Josh can answer.

"The boyfriend." She chews on her pen for about two seconds. "Come with me. Both of you."

In the hall, she flags down a young man. "Jared, take the boyfriend to makeup."

"What?" Josh says. "No, I'm just—" But Jared has grabbed his hand and is leading him somewhere opposite of where I'm going. I shrug at Josh, who gives me his smile.

They told me to come with my hair washed and my face plain. It was weird, because I usually at least wear some concealer, but here I am naked-faced. They sit me in a chair and pin my hair up to start working on my face. There are three people with various brushes and colors.

"I know I have brown hair and seem to be an autumn, but really I think I'm more of a—"

"SHHHH!" one of them says to me and puts her finger to my lips. "It's important not to talk while we work." She has what I think is a Russian accent. "Makes your face muscles move, and we might highlight a cheekbone up on your brow, no?"

I sit back, chagrined. I'm sure they know what to do.

It takes about an hour, maybe longer. I realize I really have to pee.

121

When it seems they are finished, I attempt to talk.

"Can I use the lady's room?"

"SHHHH!" The Russian woman says again. I'm sure she was part of the KGB at some point. She probably made people up as spies. Changed their appearance. They've kept me turned around with my back to the mirror, so I have no idea how I look.

"Ethan!" she calls out after more time has passed.

Some man dressed in very loud clothes, who I assume is Ethan, whisks over to me and lets my hair down. It falls in a cascade around my shoulders. He begins to work.

I swear another hour has gone by. By now, I've forgotten about Myra Winnrey and can only concentrate on my bladder.

"I really have to pee," I whisper.

Ethan grunts and spins my chair around so I can face the mirror.

I'm stunned. I'm gorgeous. I have no idea what they did, because my makeup is subtle and my hair is just–down. It's just loosely down around my shoulders but fuller, shinier, and just...gorgeous. I am gorgeous.

"What do you think?" Ethan asks.

"I, uh...wow." It's all I can say. Words are escaping me.

Ethan nods, and I can tell he's pleased. "Thank you," he says. Then he gestures off to the right with his comb. "Ladies restrooms that way."

OhthankyouGod.

I hasten to the bathroom and empty my bladder. Then it's on to wardrobe, and someone has ironed my outfit that I brought to wear. An ironer. I have an ironer.

I think that's what I need at home. Someone to iron for me. I'll hire her, and she (or he) can come in once a week and just iron. Come to think of it, I can actually afford to do that. Why am I not living the life of the rich and famous?

I put my outfit on, and it's nearly time. They pull me into something called the "Green Room," which isn't green at all. I sit on the couch and wait, clutching the magazine I brought. A woman comes in and dusts my cheeks one more time. Then Josh walks in.

Oh my gosh. If I thought he was hot before...

They've done something to his hair, with some gel or something, and it's kind of swooped back, leaving his curls but adding a sort of wave. He is still wearing his jeans but they've changed him into a T-shirt that…well, let's just say it's tighter than the one he was wearing before, and it really shows off his arms. For a moment, all I want to do is stare, and then it dawns on me that millions of viewers are going to see *my* man and his bulging biceps. I feel a bit of irritation. Is it jealously? It's not like we're exclusive…or are we?

Maybe we need to be. It had never occurred to me before to think of competition.

Where is my mind wandering? I have to pull myself together.

"Hi," I say.

Josh says, "I'm really not comfortable—"

"You'll be fine," says the woman who escorted him in. She's brushing some powder on his face. Then she straightens his shirt a bit. Why is she touching him?

"I'm not prepared to go on television," he continues. "This was just supposed to be Amy."

"You're on in five," the woman says and leaves.

Five. As in *minutes*?

"Wait. What? Don't I get to look at a list of questions first?" I say.

But the woman scurries out. I hear the music signaling that Myra's show is about to start.

I glance over at Josh. "Nice shirt," I say.

"Yeah, uh…" This is the first time I've ever seen him uncomfortable. "Wasn't I good enough the way I arrived?" He gives a little laugh.

"Nice arms," I say and give him a wink. He laughs.

"Amy, you look amazing, as ever."

"Thanks," I move over to him and squeeze his hand. "Thank you for coming on stage with me. I'm scared to death."

"It's not like they gave me a choice. They just moved me along and didn't let me speak."

Myra is live on the air now, telling viewers and the live audience about the guests on today's show. A man comes from onstage and ushers Josh and me over to the stage door where we can see her.

"First off today is a woman who is tired of trying to be perfect," says Myra. "No more fad diets for her. No more designer clothes. No more trying to claw her way up to the top of the corporate ladder. She's decided that she is good enough the way she is. And so are you. So we've brought her on today to discuss her amazing new magazine, *Good Enough*. With her is her sexy and supportive boyfriend. Welcome to Amy Summers and Josh Gray."

The crowd breaks out in thunderous applause, and the stage manager gives me a little push. I walk out onto the stage and wave like I've seen Myra's guests do on her show. Then I take the seat on the couch closest to her. Josh follows me out, smiling that amazing smile of his. He sits down next to me.

"Welcome Amy and Josh," says Myra. I can't believe I'm sitting here. HERE. Next to Myra Winnrey on her show. On live television.

Myra leans over, takes my magazine, and holds it up for the viewers to see. I really do like the cover. I'll have to thank my graphics people again when I get back. She talks a bit about some of the things coming up in our December issue and then places it on a stand on a table next to her so the cover shows to the viewing audience.

"So tell us how this idea came about," says Myra. I go back to meeting Josh in a coffee shop and discussing what I'd like to do with my life. And how I found this job as a consultant, shared my ideas, and became the editor.

"But that's not all you are," says Myra, with a wink. "You're the woman behind the magazine, aren't you?"

"What?"

"The owner. We did a little digging. Second Chances is owned by you, Ms. Summers." Myra gives a little wag of her index finger. "You're way more than the editor."

I'm stunned. I've been trapped on live television. Who *is* this woman? This can't be the same feel-good Myra Winnrey who gives cars away to her audience, feeds orphans in India by donating $1 million in cash on live TV, and gives puppies to small children at a New York clinic? (The television coverage of the kids hugging those puppies made me bawl like a baby.) Myra is looking at me, waiting for a response. I laugh. "I think you're mistaken about that." "No, we're quite sure we're not," says Myra. "So tell us, why Second Chances?"Josh clears his throat. "Amy is big in believing in second chances, which is why she'll be printing essays from at-risk youth at Girl's Town next spring and pairing them up with mentors in fields they are interested in." "Really?" says Myra, interested. "Tell me more." God bless this man. I concentrate on my breathing while Josh fills her in on the essay project. "That's truly amazing," says Myra. "Let our show know if we can help in any way. So let's talk about the December issue. Tell us about the photo on the cover." Here's where I'm good. I talk about how we want women to be empowered by the talents they already have and to stop comparing themselves to others. We are all created differently, with our own special gifts. Whether yours is to bag groceries and be pleasant to your customers, run a multi-million dollar business, or stay at home and raise the next generation, you should feel empowered doing your best in your situation. That's all we can be, our best. "There's always room to learn and to grow," I add. "And I'm all for higher education and all of that, but I think we need to quit beating ourselves up and over-packing our schedule just so we can do more and be more. When is enough, enough?" The crowd applauds, and I smile. I casually try to lean on the couch's armrest, but that's when I discover it doesn't have one. My elbow hits air, and I almost fall off. But no one seems to notice. Josh does reach over and take my hand. "So, Josh. What do you do for a living?" Josh tells about being a life coach. "And he's an amazing builder and woodworker," I add. "Well, Amy, it looks like you've got it all together," Myra says, "including a great boyfriend." The music starts to play, and Myra says, "Stick around, folks. When we come back, we're going to have Amy size up

125

a few of our audience members who have been feeling down and explain to them why they are good enough as they are."

The music gets louder, somebody says "off air," and Myra smiles over at me.

"What? Nobody told me we were going to do that." I laugh nervously.

"It was a last-minute decision," says Myra. "We asked our audience members if they were dissatisfied with their lives. If so, they were to fill out a card. We randomly selected a few, and we want you to tell them why they're okay. It'll be fine. You have 60 seconds per person."

Sixty seconds?

Someone comes out and puts some powder on all of our faces, leaving Josh coughing. Then there's music again, and before I know it, I'm back on live television. The audience applauds on cue (someone holds up a sign that says *Applause*), and we're on again.

Myra explains the audience member participation and brings the first one on stage.

"From Connecticut, we have this young mother with five children under age seven." A wispy woman with dark circles under her eyes appears. "Her sister gave her tickets to today's show as a gift, so this is one of her first outings in seven years. She says she's exhausted and wants to know if the housework will ever end. She wrote on her card 'I love being a mom, but sometimes I wish I had never left my job as a career analyst.'"

The woman *looks* exhausted. I want to take her home, put her to bed, and let her stay there for a week.

"Amy, tell her why she's good enough," says Myra. Then she sits back with a smile and all the confidence in the world.

"Um..." I begin. I know nothing about motherhood. Nothing. I'm going to have to wing this and then, oh boy, is Myra going to hear it from me when this show is over. "Well..." I stall for time. Someone holds up a sign that only I can see. It reads *60 seconds!!*

I take a deep breath. "What's your name?" I ask.

"Jennie."

"Jennie, you are doing the world's most important job right now. You are raising our country's next generation of workers and parents and citizens. If you can raise them with integrity, selflessness, and love, then you've done your job. I'm only here today because I had good parents who encouraged me. And as far as the career analyst job you had, you will definitely be able to multi-task better, analyze people more clearly, and dish out knowledge that comes from living a life of difficult days and many choices from your current situation. When you get back into the work force, you'll be a heck of a catch."

I exhale. Jennie beams. I did it. "You're right, of course," she says. "I just needed to hear someone else say it." She comes forward and gives me a hug. The crowd applauds. I can't see if it's because of the applause sign or not, but I don't care. I'm happy.

"Amy, thank you. You are a natural," says Myra. "Next up is a computer programmer from New Jersey who works long hours. He says art is his first dream, but everyone tells him not to give up his day job to chase a dream because artists starve and loft space is too expensive."

He is thin and ghostly pale. He definitely needs to get outdoors.

"Your name?" I ask.

"Cliff."

"Cliff, are you married, or do you have children?"

"No. Neither."

"Then go for it. If you think you have talent, maybe work part time or find a job where you can work fewer hours while you chase your dream. I believe with enough hard work, you can figure out your art. If you starve, it's only you that you are starving, not a family. You can always bag groceries or wait tables to pay the bills while you perfect your art. As for loft space, I'm sure where you live is good enough. You can figure out natural light. Use the space you have. Save your free time for art. Life is too short. Be who you were created to be."

"Wow. Thanks," says Cliff. He is beaming.

I'm getting the hang of this.

"Thank you, Amy," says Myra. "We have time for one last guest. From New York City, dog walker Charles is tired of being single."

Charles walks out on stage. His trousers are covered in dog hair, and he is sneezing.

"I'm allergic," he apologizes.

"To dogs?" I ask.

"Yes. But I love them. My mom tells me I should quit, but I love this job."

His mom? He looks to be in his forties.

"Well…so you want to date?"

"Yes."

They hold up the 60 seconds sign at me again.

I look at his dog-hair covered body.

"Charles, if this is what you want to do, buy yourself some antihistamines and find yourself a woman who loves dogs. I'm sure you can meet one in the park, walking her own dogs. Join a dog club or take your dogs to the dog park to play. There's bound to be like-minded women there."

"There are not," says Charles.

I hear the theme song begin to play, and we have to go to a commercial break.

"Thank you, Amy," says Myra. "And for all you single ladies out there, Charles here would love to take you on a date."

Charles beams, the music grows louder, and they cut to the commercial break. The powder lady comes back out, and Charles is escorted off the stage. "You can't win them all," Myra whispers to me. "You did good enough." She laughs, and we are pulled off stage and handed the copy of the magazine. Before I know it, it's over, and Myra's next guest is getting ready to come in. He's a chef from Paraguay who opened his own restaurant in New York featuring all organic food.

Back in the Green Room, we shut the door. "What happened?" Josh asks as he pulls me into a hug. "What was all of that? It was so fast, and there were bright lights and people clapping."

I laugh and hug him back. "I'm so glad that's over!" I say truthfully. It'll take me a while to process what just happened in fifteen minutes onstage. I can't wait to see the program. My parents are taping it.

My parents. Drat. There's that part about me owning the magazine.

"Thanks for covering for me out there," I say to Josh.

"Always," he says. "But you didn't need me. You did great." He gives me a kiss. "Our plane doesn't leave for several more hours," he says. "I have a surprise for you."

"Really? What?"

"If I told you, it wouldn't be a surprise."

I change into the jeans I brought along for the flight home, and Josh puts his own T-shirt back on and pulls on a sweater. When our driver picks us up, Josh asks him to take us to Central Park. When we get there, he asks the driver to stick around for a while and tells me to leave my bags in the car.

"We're going ice skating," he says.

"Ice skating?" I haven't ice skated since I was a kid. But it's a great day for it, and a light snow has just started falling. The ice rink looks magical. There are all of these people out there, laughing, and music is coming from a speaker somewhere. Josh takes my hand and leads me over to the skate rental place. We get our skates and put them on. It's cold, but I'm glad I brought jeans and have my winter coat.

Then Josh takes my hand. I'm very wobbly and almost fall as soon as I get on the ice, but he puts his arm around my waist.

"I've got you," he says. He starts off slowly, his arm supporting me. He's really good and very balanced.

"Where did you learn to skate?" I ask.

"I used to play hockey," he said. "Scott and I."

"Oh."

We skate around the rink, Josh with his arm around me. I soon get the hang of it, and remember how to turn and stop. We switch to holding hands, and around and around we go. There are trees lining the rink and a curved bridge we can skate under. Behind us is the backdrop of New York's buildings. It's magical, and I see a few horses pulling a white carriage to add to the charm.

When it's time to go, we're both tired and I'm out of breath.

We sit down and start unlacing our skates.

"That was so fun!" I say, and Josh agrees. Some snowflakes have stuck to his long eyelashes. I start to brush them off, but realize my gloves are covered in snow, and I am only leaving more snow on his face.

We laugh again, and he pulls me onto his lap and gives me another kiss.

"We've gotta go," he says, and I realize what time it is. We run to our car, and our driver speeds us off to the airport.

At the terminal, Josh buys us both some hot chocolate and sandwiches, which we eat on the plane. I'm famished.

In the cab back to my apartment, I text my parents and Andrea. I tell them all about our day and send them a few photos of Central Park. They text back with lots of emots and exclamation marks. Everybody is happy.

Josh can't stay because we took a cab, but that's okay. I'm exhausted. I'm so tired from the day and from our ice skating that I completely forget about the revelation that I own the business. I fall asleep as soon as I get home. I don't even think to take my makeup off.

And I forget about my problems.

That is, until Bart shows up at my door the next morning.

Chapter Eighteen

The buzzer on my door rings while I'm in the shower. It's insistent, so I rinse the shampoo out of my hair and, still dripping wet, pull my robe around me to go answer it, thinking maybe it's Josh.

You can imagine how shocked I am when I look through the peephole and see Bart standing there, all decked out in his suit. He always did get up early.

"Bart?" I say through the door.

"Amy, can we talk?"

"Now?"

"It's important."

I open my door. Mrs. Crabbs is standing down the hallway, smoking. She raises an eyebrow.

Bart's eyes travel up and down my body, taking in the robe and probably figuring out there is nothing on underneath. He raises his own eyebrow and nods approvingly. The scumbag.

"Amy," he says.

A myriad of emotions are swirling through me, but the one I recognize most is anger.

"What do you want?" I say.

Bart glances at Mrs. Crabbs. "Can I come in?"

"No."

Bart is always unruffled, so I don't really expect him to react to that.

"I was thinking…" Bart says. He looks me in the eye, his own eyes showing concern and compassion. "I moved too hastily. I…have feelings for you, Amy, and I don't know what I was thinking. I can't live without you. Will you have me back?"

My wet hair is dripping down the back of my robe. I am cold, and I want to get dried off and dressed.

Who does he think he is, after all he did to me?

"No."

Bart looks hurt. He always was good with the puppy-dog face.

"Why?"

"Why? WHY? Because you're a lying, cheating, stealing, awful…man. That's why. You lie. You cheat."

Bart's look of hurt turns to a look of anger.

"You!" he points a finger at me. "YOU steal too. You stole my lottery ticket."

I freeze. Mrs. Crabbs takes a long drag of her cigarette and stifles a cough.

"I what?" I say.

"You stole my lottery ticket. I've looked everywhere. My girlfriend looked everywhere. Then I saw you on Myra Winnrey yesterday. I saw how you suddenly own this big, fancy magazine, and it clicked. YOU were there that day I bought it. YOU were there that day I lost it. You must have found it and cashed it in. There's no other explanation."

"You're crazy. Second Chances owns that magazine, not me."

"Whatever. I want my money."

I'm not sure what to say, but I want to get rid of my nosy neighbor. "Mrs. Crabbs, can you please mind your own business?" I say. She scowls at me, but stubs out her cigarette and goes back inside her apartment.

"Your *girlfriend?*" I said. "I thought you came over here to get back together with me."

"Former girlfriend. And I don't want you. I want my money. Which you have."

"I have a job as the editor of that magazine. That's it."

"Amy, I'm a lawyer. I know you own it. You're lying."

We're in a stalemate, eyes locked on each other. I'm so angry I want to hit him with something, but part of me is also afraid. Can he prove it? Could he sue me?

"Get out," I say. "Get out before I call the police."

Thankfully, Mrs. Burgess must have heard the conversation. (Our doors are really thin.) She opens her door.

"I have my cell phone right here," she says, holding it up as proof. "If you don't leave this young lady alone right now, I'm calling 911."

Bart spins to look at her. She pushes "9" on the dial pad. He turns back to me. "This isn't over. I know you have my money, and somehow I'll prove it."

He turns to leave and stomps out of the building.

"Thank you, Mrs. Burgess," I say. My heart is pounding.

"Are you okay, dear?"

"Yes. I am. I've got to get ready for work."

I close the door, lean up against it, and take some slow breaths. My hands are shaking. How dare he. How dare he try to mess up my life again.

Then I start to blame myself. My stupid self for letting myself be on national television. And now I have to deal with my parents. I have to come clean about owning the magazine and how I got the money. And I probably need to call my own lawyers.

I'm starting to get a headache, but I get dressed and go into the office.

"OHMYGOSH!" squeals Suzanne as soon as I walked through the door. "You were fantastic! FANTASTIC. We all watched it together on the TV in the break room. You looked really pretty, and Josh, we didn't expect to see him on there!"

"I don't think he expected to be on there!" I say, laughing.

There are flowers on my desk.

"Harlan brought those in," Suzanne says. "They were here when I got here this morning."

I read the card. "To Amy, who makes dreams come true."

I sigh and sit down.

"Amy, are you okay? You look like you've seen a ghost," says Suzanne. She brings me a coffee. That's not part of her job, but I guess she can see how shaken I am.

"My ex visited me this morning. He showed up at my apartment, and I wasn't even dressed. I had just gotten out of the shower."

"Oh, how awful," Suzanne pulls a chair over to my desk and sits down. "I know if my ex ever sees me again, I want to look so hot he'll regret the day he left me. Left us, little Marcus and me," she adds. She stares wistfully into space.

"Some men suck," I say.

"They do," Suzanne says. "Why did he stop by?"

I sigh, not sure how to answer this question. Finally, I say, "He thought I had something of his. He wanted it back. At first, he said he wanted *me* back. Hah. Not that I would have taken him back."

"The jerk."

"Yes."

My cell phone rings. It's my mom. "We can dis ex-boyfriends later," Suzanne says and leaves me to answer my phone.

Mom squeals as soon as I pick the phone up.

"You were on TV! My baby girl was on TV!" she says.

I laugh. "I was sitting right there next to Myra! Did you see when I almost fell off the couch?"

"Oh honey, nobody noticed that," Mom says. "You were wonderful. So was Josh."

"Thanks, Mom."

There's a long pause while I pray she doesn't ask about me owning the company.

"Honey, can we have lunch?" she says.

"Today?" I glance at my calendar.

"Yes."

"Um…"

I still have to tell Josh about the lottery ticket. He needs to be first. And now I've got this problem with Bart. My stomach is starting to feel queasy.

"Dad and I can come down there," Mom says. "We want to talk to you, honey."

Drat. She's going to ask.

"Okay," I say reluctantly. "Pick me up around 11. We'll go to Annie's Café."

"Great. See you then." Mom blows a kiss into the phone and hangs up.

I need to talk to Josh first.

As if on cue, he texts me.

Got a minute?

Yep.

He calls. "I have to go out of town overnight," he says. "One of my clients, the Richard guy I was telling you about, had a heart attack and wants me to be there when he presents his children with his new will. He thinks he's going to die this week, but the doctor says no. Anyway, he and I worked hard to figure out his future and what he should do with his money. I think I need to be there. It's urgent to him."

"Okay," I say. "When will you go?"

"I'm leaving in an hour. We're meeting this afternoon, just he and I, at the hospital where he was admitted. Then his children are coming in in the morning."

"Okay. I didn't know life coaches did end-of-life things," I say.

"We don't." I can hear the smile in his voice. "Richard is the only one who thinks this is the end of his life. I've been working with him for over a year, so I feel kind of responsible for his life choices. I'll be home tomorrow night, and we can get together then."

"I love you," I say.

"I love you too."

After he hangs up, I realize I won't be able to tell him before I meet up with my parents.

It's a busy morning. The December issue comes out today and within hours we are getting calls to print more. Sales have tripled from last month, most likely due to Myra Winnrey's show yesterday, I'm sure. We are suddenly a national magazine, on the newsstands and in grocery store checkout lanes around the country.

People start calling with story ideas.

"I can't handle all of these phone calls!" Suzanne says at 10:30. "It's insane. We're getting distributors calling demanding more magazines, people calling to place ads in upcoming issues, and story ideas coming in by phone and internet. I can't keep up with the emails either!" Suzanne looks frustrated for the first time since I've met her. Her hair is even out of place.

"I'll help. I'll answer the emails. You handle the phones and send me the second line."

And so we start. There are tons of emails zipping in, but I can't get to them because the phone won't stop ringing. When my parents arrive at 11 a.m., I barely have time to look up.

"Mom, we're way understaffed," I say. "I can't do lunch."

Mom takes one look at me and then at Suzanne out in the lobby. "Let me help," she says. I briefly bring her up to date on what's happening, and Mom sits at my desk and takes over the phone while I start categorizing emails. Some are really important because they are coming from people who want to advertise with us, which means income. And some of the stories I'm getting are heart breaking. There are so many hurting women out there, women who have tried their whole lives to be something they are not.

We don't even stop for lunch. By the time 5 p.m. rolls around and we send the phones to voice mail, Suzanne, my mom and I are exhausted and hoarse. Dad disappeared long ago into the sales room to help Mark take notes.

I collapse back into my chair and sigh.

"We need to hire help," says Suzanne. "Mark needs help in sales."

"We need another writer too," I say.

We discuss our needs and then Josh calls.

"Do you want me to put ads in?" he offers. "I can do that tonight from my laptop in the hotel room."

"Will you?" He did a marvelous job the last time, helping me staff the magazine.

"Of course."

Mom has left to go find food, so Josh and I talk a bit. He tells me about his day after I finish telling him about mine. When we hang up, I realize I'm starved and my shoulders are hurting from spending too much time at the computer and on the phone.

"Dinner," Mom says, bringing in some Chinese take-out.

Suzanne has left with Marcus, and the others are gone. It's 7 p.m., and I'm alone with my parents.

Alone with my parents.

Oh my gosh. I've got to get out of here. But suddenly my body is tired of running, and my mind is tired of lies.

Dad scoops out some sweet and sour pork onto his rice. He smiles across at me.

"Tough day," he says.

"Yes." I remember it all started with Bart at my apartment. That seems so long ago.

"So..." Mom says, then pauses to scoop some lo mien onto her paper plate.

"Mom, Dad, yes there are things I need to tell you," I say. My eyes fill with tears. It has been a long, emotional week with Myra, the trip to New York, Bart, and then all of the success of today. What I want more than anything right now is to feel Josh's arms around me. And maybe to sleep.

I'm so tired, I could sleep right here at my desk.

"But I need to tell Josh first," I say. "Can you trust me just a little bit longer? I'll tell you everything, I promise. But he deserves to know first."

My parents look across my desk at me for a moment. Then Dad gives me that smile he always gave me when I was little and had just asked if I could climb up on his lap for a bedtime story. I almost think he's going to reach over and ruffle my hair.

"Of course, honey," he says.

"We trust you, Amy. We're just worried about you," says Mom.

I smile. "I know you are. I can tell you that I'm not an alcoholic. Or in recovery from any drugs for that matter. I was there with a friend, Harlan, who will be coming in here any minute to clean the place. He's our janitor. He was celebrating his 30-day anniversary and wanted me to be there to see him get his award."

Then it occurs to me that anonymous is in the name for a reason. I shouldn't have mentioned who my friend was.

But these are my parents. The people I trust most in the entire world.

Mom laughs. "I thought it must be something like that," she says. "You never were one to get into much trouble."

If only she knew.

"Okay," Mom agrees. "Tell us when you're ready. Just please tell us."

"We all believe in second chances," Dad says, and winks. I smile. Then we hear the door open, and Harlan comes in.

"I'm heading home," I say, standing up and picking up my keys. "I'm beat. Finish your dinner. Harlan will lock the door when you leave."

I kiss my parents goodbye and head outside into the cool night air. I want to go home to my cat and my simple apartment, reminders of my life before, when I didn't have this constant knot in my stomach.

Tomorrow. I will tell Josh tomorrow.

Chapter Nineteen

Josh ends up staying longer with his client Richard. Apparently, Richard has a lot of money to throw around and puts Josh up in a hotel. Josh's boss wants him to follow through until Richard feels comfortable. That won't happen until Richard is released.

But the weekend goes by quickly because I have a ton of things to do, like grocery shopping, laundry, and just the stuff of life. I don't hear from Bart again and begin to wonder if he will just leave it all alone.

On Monday, Suzanne brings in a list of people who are applying for the jobs we posted.

I immediately recognize a name. "Lydia!" I say. Lydia was one of the writers at InterFind. I really liked her, and she was an excellent writer, winning all sorts of awards for our website copy. Sometimes, when she went out of town, I got to step away from ad writing to write a little website copy and add things to our blog. But mainly that was Lydia's job.

"I used to work with her. She's awesome." I pass the list back to Suzanne. "Call her in first."

Lydia comes in on her lunch hour. The thing about Lydia is that she doesn't look normal. She has various body parts pierced and wears her hair spiked. But she's an incredible writer. I still read her personal blog on social reform, even though I'm not really interested in social reform.

"I'm bored," she says when I ask why she wants to leave InterFind. "I wanted to do journalism, and this magazine will give me so much more of a chance to do that."

So I hire her. Later that afternoon, I decide on another salesperson, and we hire him.

To help Suzanne with the temporary increase in phone calls and emails, I hire her a temp.

The next few days go by quickly because we're getting them settled in.

Suzanne and I are also putting the finishing touches on the holiday party. We're having it this Saturday. There's still a lot to do.

I've rented the ballroom downtown at the Glory Bee. It's an old, vintage hotel decorated in beautiful colors of gold and red. They have the place all decked out for Christmas.

There's going to be a lavish buffet, and I've hired a band to play some dinner music and then perform afterwards so we can do some dancing. I'm so excited about it all!

Richard is finally released from the hospital, and Josh comes home on Thursday.

"Let's celebrate your successes," Josh says, showing up at my office and whisking me out of the office early that December evening. We hug and kiss, and it feels so good when he wraps his arms around me. I can't believe how much I missed him.

"Richard is happy and all settled back at home," Josh says. "He did give us a scare two nights ago. We all thought his heart had stopped, but it was only that his monitor fell off."

I laugh, happy to be alive and happy that Richard has more time on this earth, even though I've never met him.

Josh and I go out to eat at our favorite restaurant, right across from the magazine. We are seated at a table by the window, which he apparently called ahead for.

"What? People don't make reservations here," I say as the waiter seats us.

Josh smiles across the table at me, and for a moment I'm lost in those amazing eyes.

"Look," he says gently, and points across the street. From our table, we can see the big evergreen wreath with small white lights hanging up on our third floor, and the tiny lights across the top of the building.

I gasp. Josh must have had it put up there this afternoon while I was away at a meeting. I've been so busy, I forgot all about wanting one.

"Josh…" I'm too happy to speak.

"Remember when we first came here? You were dreaming about how beautiful it would look and how you wanted to hang a wreath up there? I called Suzanne and we worked it out."

"It's…it's perfect," I say, because it is. It's exactly how I imagined it last spring when we first came here to look at the building I had just bought. So much has happened so fast. "It's so pretty," I say. A soft snow is falling now, softening the lights just a little bit. It's magical.

"It is beautiful," Josh says. He reaches across the table and takes my hand. "Just like you."

I smile. Josh compliments me a lot. He's always sincere, and I never get tired of hearing it.

Then he pulls a little box out of his pocket. It's pencil-length and wrapped in gold foil with a red ribbon.

"I got you an early Christmas present," he says.

I slowly take the box. It looks about the size of a necklace box. I'm wondering if he got me some jewelry.

I smile up at him.

"Open it," he says.

I pull at the ribbon and it comes undone. Then I take the lid off the box, and what I see surprises me. Inside, lying on a piece of green velvet, is a wooden pen. I pick it up, and it's smooth and soft against my fingers. It seems to be made of cherry wood and has a gold clip on the side. I turn it over in my hand and see that it's inscribed. "Once upon a time…" There is also a small engraved heart.

"You can make up the rest of the story," Josh says. "And I hope I'm in it until the end."

It's beautiful. It's quite frankly the most beautiful thing I've ever received.

"Did you make this?" I ask.

"Yes, I did."

"It's beautiful. I love it. It's perfect."

I lean across the table and kiss him. His lips are soft, and I grasp his warm hands in mine. "You'll always be part of my story," I say.

And I hope that's true. Josh is my happily ever after. I'm sure of it.

After dinner, we go shopping, and I pick up a few things for my parents and my new nephew for Christmas. It's fun to shop for babies, and Josh and I have a blast picking out stuffed animals, bibs with funny sayings on them, and some cute little baby-sized Nike booties.

The night is so perfect that I don't want to bring up the lottery ticket. Not tonight.

"What do you want for Christmas?" Josh asks.

"Just you," I turn to him. We're in the Michigan store now, and I've just had a cherry pie boxed up for me. He pulls me into his arms, and we kiss, right there in front of the cashier. She rings me up, and I have to break away from Josh to sign the receipt.

"You already have me," he says. "What else do you want?"

"What else do I need?" I say playfully. I ask him what he wants.

"I already have what I want," he says and pulls me into his arms again. I laugh, and we kiss some more.

My handmade pen is tucked inside my coat pocket, and I feel it press against me as he holds me. There's Christmas music playing somewhere down the street, and a soft snow is falling around us, glistening in the light of the street lamps and against the frosted glass of the storefronts. It's a perfect magical, mystical, Christmassy night.

Chapter Twenty

Suzanne comes into my office early the next day with roses in her hand. She sets them on my desk.

"You look so happy," she says.

I look at the card. They're from Josh.

"I am," I say. I can't hide my smile.

She stands there a minute and then asks, "Did your ex ever come back for what he wanted?"

I glance at her. "No." I say. Thank goodness. I hadn't heard back from Bart so far. I had almost forgotten about it.

She sighs.

"The money that I thought my ex was putting into a trust for Marcus. It's yours, isn't it?"

I look up startled. "Um..."

"It has to be," Suzanne says. "I confronted my ex the other day because he came snooping around to see if I had any money." She gives a short, humorless laugh. "Which I don't, and I thanked him for setting up the trust. But it wasn't him, the jerk. I should have known. And there is nobody else. So it has to be you."

She watches me for a moment, and I take a drink of my coffee to stall for time. But I'm tired of lying.

"Yes," I say.

She just stares at me for a moment. "Why?" she finally asks softly.

"Because nobody should have to grow up without a father," I say. "Your ex is a jerk, and I want Marcus to be okay. And Suzanne, you've been such a help to me, and I just want you both to be okay."

Tears come to Suzanne's eyes. "Amy...I don't even know what to say."

"Thank you?"

We both laugh.

"Yes!" she says. "Thank you!" She comes around the desk and gives me a hug. She goes back around my desk and is about to leave when she turns again.

"You know, Amy, I'm so happy here. I was thinking last night, if I hadn't lost that lottery ticket, I'd be married to that jerk by now and would have never met you. Isn't it weird how things turn out?"

My heart sinks.

"Suzanne..."

"Yes?"

But I want to tell Josh first. I should have told him last night. Stupid me.

She is standing there, waiting. Waiting for what I want her to do. She's amazing like that, and I'm a stupid, lying, awful person.

"Nothing..." I say. My voice trails off. She frowns for a moment.

"Are you okay?" she asks.

"Yes," I say. "I was just thinking about some regrets I have and how if I hadn't made certain choices, I wouldn't be here either. Sometimes it's hard to know if what we're doing is the right thing."

"It is at the time," she says. "But later, that's when you know. You can look back and see how it all worked out. Or didn't."

"Hindsight is 20/20," I say. She agrees.

"Suzanne?"

"Hmmm?"

"Let's do a long lunch together on Monday. Just you and me. I have some things I want to talk to you about."

"Okay," she says brightly. "I'll put it on your calendar."

She leaves. I sit alone in my office, thinking. I have it all worked out. Tomorrow night is the Christmas party. I'll tell Josh after the party, when we're alone at home. I'll tell my parents Sunday and then Suzanne on Monday. It's only right.

I look around the office, for what will probably be my last full day of work. After I confess about the lottery ticket, I'll lose it all. It's not mine to keep.

I run my hand along the wood of my office desk and turn my nameplate around.

Amy Summers, Editor.

It should be changed to Amy Summers, Liar.

I phone my parents and set up a lunch date with them Sunday. I'll come clean this weekend, and then on Monday, I'll give Suzanne her money.

Then it'll all be over.

The next day, I'm a nervous wreck about talking to Josh, but I get dressed in the little red dress I bought and put my hair up. Josh picks me up and I give him a quick kiss.

We drive to the Glory Bee. It's a beautiful, old hotel/banquet facility. They've decorated the room brilliantly. The lighting is low, with candles on all the tables and in some of the wall sconces. There's a DJ playing some soft Christmas music. Dinner is buffet style with lasagna, roast beef, and potatoes. There are salads, rolls, and various pastries for dessert. I choose a chocolate brownie torte and eat the whole thing. It's nervous eating. I'm so nervous about telling Josh that I can't enjoy my evening.

"Amy, are you okay?" Josh asks several times. I nod. "It's just excitement," I say.

The DJ starts up some dance music, and we watch from our table as some of our work colleagues get into the groove of things with the song "Celebration." They play a few more fast songs before a slow song comes on. Josh takes my hand.

"Will you dance with me?" he asks.

As he puts his arms around me on the dance floor, I lay my head on his shoulders and forget about things for a while. I start to relax. I wish I could stay here forever, in Josh's arms, safe and loved. This is where I belong.

After the dance, I'm standing beside Josh, who has his arm around me, when Lydia comes over to introduce herself to him. He smiles and shakes her hand, and then Suzanne joins us.

Lydia has been drinking a bit and is somewhat tipsy.

"This one is much better than the last one," she says to me.

"What?" I say.

She points to Josh with her glass of wine. "Josh, here. He's much better than Bart."

"Um…yes, he is," I say. I start to pull Josh away when Lydia grabs my arm. "Which reminds me, he was poking around here yesterday," she says. "When you were at that meeting."

I swallow. "He was?"

"Said something about you stealing his lottery ticket. And that's why you had all of this money."

"Money? I don't have…"

"Wait. A lottery ticket? That sounds like *my* ex," says Suzanne.

"Yes, it must have been hers," I say.

"No, it was definitely Bart. I know Bart," Lydia laughs. "You and I have been out together as couples. And don't forget the work parties at InterFind. I know what Bart looks like."

"Bart?" Suzanne gives me a look. "Bart thinks *you* have my lottery ticket?"

Lydia narrows her eyes and leans in toward me, almost splashing some of her wine on my dress. "Where *did* you get all of this money, Amy?" Lydia asks. "When you worked at InterFind, you drove that little car and lived in that tiny apartment."

"She still does." Josh laughs, but he's uneasy.

"I, uh…"

"Wait. You dated Bart too?" Suzanne says.

It's all falling apart. Suddenly the room seems to be closing in on me, and I'm feeling woozy. Suzanne is staring at me, her mouth open.

"Excuse me," I say. I pull my arm away from Josh and head toward the women's bathroom.

Josh follows me.

"Amy?" he asks. "What's all of this about?"

I'm hyperventilating. I try taking some deep breaths to calm myself. I feel tears come to my eyes. This is not how I wanted Josh to find out.

I turn to him. "It's true," I say. I pull him aside, over near the stairs where there are no people.

"I found my ex's lottery ticket, and I kept it. Later, I found out it wasn't his, but Suzanne's. But I didn't know that until long after the magazine was started and–"

"You cashed in a lottery ticket?" Josh said. "Is that where you got the money?"

I don't respond.

"Your aunt didn't will you money?"

"Josh–"

"You lied to me."

He lets go of my arm and takes a step backwards. I see a look of hurt in his eyes.

"No, I just–"

"You not only lied to me, but you've been lying to me for months," Josh says. "*Months.*"

I don't know what to say. It's true. I have. And not only to him, but to my parents. And Suzanne.

"Who else knows?" he demands.

"Nobody." My voice is small.

Josh's eyes are suddenly hard, angry. Without another word, he turns and walks away.

"Josh, wait," I call out to him. Without looking back, he grabs his coat from the rack and heads outside, closing the door behind him.

I grab my own coat and take off outside after him, but I see him getting into a cab.

"Josh, wait!" I cry out, but he either doesn't hear me or he ignores me.

I'm standing there, tears rolling down my cheeks, when another cab stops near me.

"Lady, you need a ride someplace?" a man asks. I nod and get in the cab, and he takes me home to my apartment.

Chapter Twenty-One

I try to contact Josh by texts and phone calls, but he isn't answering. Finally, around 2 a.m., I fall asleep on the couch, still in my red dress.

When I wake up around 8 a.m., I realize it's Sunday and my life is a mess, and I pull the blanket over my head and go back to sleep.

At 10 a.m., I get off the couch and check my phone. Nothing. So I force myself to shower and get ready for lunch with my parents. Might as well get this over with too.

They're waiting for me at the café we picked. "Amy, what's wrong?" Mom says right away. I've put on makeup, but I can't hide the fact that I've been crying. My eyes and nose are all red.

"I'll tell you everything," I say.

And I do. After we order some strong coffee and our breakfasts.

I tell them the whole story, beginning with seeing Bart at the gas station and what happened after that. I tell them how I've let everyone down, lied to them both, and kept secrets from Suzanne because I didn't trust her. And now I've lost Josh.

Money really is the root of all evil.

"Oh, honey," Mom says through my weeping, because I've started crying again. "It's okay. Dad and I still love you."

Of course, they do. But nobody else does. I'm probably going to jail. Suzanne is probably going to press charges.

But what do I care? I've lost the only man I've ever loved.

Then suddenly a text beeps in from Josh. My heart jumps.

"Hold on, Mom. It's from Josh." I read it.

I thought I had finally met someone with integrity. Guess not. I can't see you any more, Amy, because I can't trust you. It was fun while it lasted. Good luck with everything.

I surprise myself by not crying again. I show the text to my parents and then put my phone back in my purse. I got what I deserved.

"Just give him some time," Mom says. "You've really hurt him."

"I know." I say. And I do. I think back on all the times I could have told him about the lottery ticket. What was I so afraid of?

Then I think of Suzanne. I guess she really wasn't spying on me. She honestly didn't know.

I wonder briefly if I've lost my mind and become a paranoid schizophrenic overnight.

After lunch, my parents ask if I want to come over, but really, I just want to be alone. I go home and change into some comfy jeans and a sweatshirt. I give Mouser some treats, and then I sit down on the couch to read a book and get my mind off my life for a while.

Then I see the drawer in the side table and pull it out. There's my gift to Bart. The watch, engraved. I take it out and read it. *Bart...loving you for two years...looking forward to a lifetime! Love, Amy*

I remember how excited I was that night, believing he was about to propose to me. What was I thinking? Bart and I didn't really have anything in common, and we didn't enjoy each other. Not like Josh and I do. Bart and I were always busy, always going to social events and stuff, but we never really talked. And I don't think Bart ever treasured me. Not like Josh does. Or did.

I have learned so much over the past year. Now I know that I don't have to settle, because I think that's what I was doing with Bart. I was settling. I didn't have a clue what it was like to really love someone and to have that someone really love me like I was the best thing that ever happened to him.

Now I do. Now I know, and I'm going to put the information to use.

I know I'm good enough. I know that I can do amazing things, like start up a magazine, which means that I can right some of the wrongs I've done to the people I care about. I'm not going to sit here and mope. I'm going to be the best person I can be, and I don't need Myra Winnrey's book to show me how to do that. I've learned it simply by living life.

So I dress smartly in one of my best suits, and I call my lawyer, because I have a plan.

I'm sitting in the restaurant across from my building, because that's where Suzanne said she wanted to meet when she called me this afternoon while I was meeting with my lawyer. "We need to talk," is what she said.

My lawyer was kind enough to open up his office on a Sunday, so I'm ready for Suzanne now. It's about 7 p.m. and is dark. There's a light snow falling, and the wreath on my building is lit up in white lights, which are blurred through the snow. It's really pretty.

Suzanne arrives and takes off her coat, shaking the snow out of her hair. She rubs her hands together to warm them and sits down without saying anything. We both order tea. Then she looks across the table at me.

"After you left the party last night, I was really upset," Suzanne says. "So I went up to the bar and ordered a martini. Then I sat there, sipped it, and looked around. There was Harlan, sitting at a table, all dressed up, and visiting with some people. He is cleaned up, Amy, and sober. He has friends and has just signed a lease on an apartment. Did you know that?"

I shake my head. I didn't.

"Then I got a text from my babysitter that Marcus was sleeping, and I could stay later if I wanted to. Marcus. The baby who has everything because you set up a trust for him.

"There were a lot of happy people at that party, Amy, because of you. People you have helped. The director of Girls Town was there, and I thought of all the girls you are planning on helping."

Suzanne takes a deep breath.

"So then I went to confront my ex. *Our* ex," she says. "Amy, I had no idea he was seeing you when we were together. He never told me. He had some story about going into Detroit to help inner city people with law issues, and I guess whenever he was doing that was when he was with you. I had no idea. Really, I didn't." Suzanne says. Her eyes are pleading. "I need for you to believe that."

I look at her, at this woman I've grown to love. She has been nothing but gracious and helpful to me. I was awful to her. And here she is worried about how *I* feel toward *her.*

"I'm sorry," I say. "In the beginning, I thought the lottery ticket belonged to Bart."

"And it would have served him right if you kept the money after he cheated on you," Suzanne says.

A tear escapes down my cheek.

"I've ruined everything," I say. "I've spent a lot of your money, I've lied to people I care about, and I've lost Josh."

"You've lost Josh?"

I tell her the story.

Suzanne shakes her head. "He'll come around."

I remember how much he talked about honesty and integrity. "I don't know," I say.

Suzanne puts her hand on my shoulder. "We'll work this out," she says.

"I already have," I say. I pull out the papers my lawyer wrote up that afternoon. "I'd like to bring you in as an equal partner," I say. "As co-owner of Second Chances." I hand her the papers, which she scans.

"Wow," she says.

"If that's not okay, I'll sell the building and everything and give you the money. But this has been so much fun, and we work well together."

"We do."

"And the rest of the money is in the bank. There's a lot left," I laugh. "It's yours, I guess."

"No," Suzanne says. "*Half* of it is mine. You keep half. You've done more with it than I ever would have done. If we're partners, then we're partners all the way."

A little over two weeks go by and Christmas arrives.

It's both the worst and the best Christmas of my life. It feels like a huge weight has been lifted since I have finally come clean about the lottery ticket. After Suzanne and I talk with more lawyers (mine, not any named Bart), we figure out that Bart didn't hold any claim over the money. We also settle that Suzanne and I will receive equal shares, which is really generous of Suzanne. But she says the same of me, since she has no legal proof that she purchased that ticket other than the fact that the numbers corresponded to her baby's birth date.

I use some of that money to buy my parents some really cool Christmas gifts.

But I can't push Josh out of my mind. He refuses to return my phone calls or texts. I haven't heard from him since that awful text he sent me that first day.

I miss him horribly. My heart hurts. I've lost some weight, and I'm not really sleeping well. But I figure that I've earned what I got. It's my fault, and there's nothing I can do to change that. There is some peace in knowing that I've done what I can.

My staff all handled the change well. I remain the editor, because Suzanne has no interest. She stays the office manager because that's what she feels she does best. And she's very good at it.

Our January issue comes out just before New Year's Day. It is called "The New You," and I have it in my hand, looking at it.

The New You. I glance at the clock on the wall. It's New Year's Eve, and I'm all alone at my desk. Suzanne has taken a vacation and won't be back for another week. It's nearly midnight.

For a moment, I think I hear the door open downstairs. I want it to be Josh, coming to give me a New Year's kiss and to tell me he has forgiven me.

But it's only the wind.

I open my drawer and take out the wooden pencil he carved for me. "Once upon a time…"

I so wish I could go back and rewrite my story.

But I can't. The clock strikes midnight, and I hear the fireworks going off outside in the streets and people cheering. I glance at my magazine cover. *The New You.*

I realize then that the past is already written, and all I have to work with is the future. Suddenly I have an idea. I put my pen to paper, and I start to write freehand all of the thoughts that come to me about new beginnings and new things. I can't make Josh come back, but I can be thankful for what I do have. This is for the February issue, which will come out very soon. In the magazine world, we are always working ahead. This month, with Valentine's Day coming up, the emphasis is on love. And here is what I write:

The Greatest of These is Love

Good Enough *magazine was created to give women a sense of self and to remind them that they are unique beings, created for a purpose, and are gifted in many different ways to make their place in the world. Whether we are writers, mothers, corporate managers, cooks, or any number of other possibilities, what matters most is that we bring integrity, honesty, and respect to those around us. But there's more we can give. And it's ours, free, given to us for the giving.*

It's called forgiveness.

There are so many times I've made mistakes and hurt those I care about. Maybe I snapped at a writer for missing a deadline. Perhaps I honked at a driver who cut me off, or I pushed past someone in the elevator. Maybe I lied about why I stayed home from work. Small misdemeanors, but still.

Then there are the larger ones. The times when we deeply hurt someone we care about.

What is driving us when we do these things? For most of us, it's not rudeness. It's fear. Fear we're going to be late. Fear we will be pushed aside if we don't stand up for ourselves. Fear we will be rejected if our true colors show.

Fear that we aren't good enough.

Love forgives. That's a quote from the world's best-selling book, The Bible. Love forgives. What I offer you this February is a challenge to look around you at those who work beside you, whether it's in the home, the office, or the factory. Look at those who interact with you—the grocery clerk, the salesman, your child's teacher, your spouse—and try to love them fully and without condition.

153

If they don't treat you with the respect you think you deserve, look deeper. Perhaps there is more going on. Perhaps there's a reason for their actions.

Forgive them.

And here's hoping, to those out there who I have hurt, that they have a big enough heart inside themselves to forgive me. I once thought I wasn't good enough, but someone showed me I was.

And I believe that now. No matter what.

- Amy

Editor in Chief

I read what I've just written, and I'm happy with it. I type it in and hit "send," and it goes off to our copyeditor, who will make sure it is put in as the "Editor's Corner" letter for our February edition.

I smile. I love the mechanics of my work and how smoothly it all falls into place.

Chapter Twenty-Two

"So you're rich," says Andrea. We're meeting for lunch during our workday at a little restaurant that's in the middle of town halfway between our offices.

I smile and stir the lemon around in my tea.

"Yes, I'm rich." This is always our first topic of conversation when we talk. She still can't believe it.

"What does it feel like?"

I take a while to answer. Actually, I'm not sure what it feels like. I've spent so many months pretending *not* to be rich that I haven't enjoyed it yet. I still live in my same apartment and drive my small-sized car. I don't own any fancy clothes, just some nice ones. I never even found someone to do my ironing.

"I don't know yet," I answer honestly. "But it is nice to be able to eat lunch today and not have to worry if I can afford it." Of course, I pay for Andrea's lunch too.

Things are going well. I was going to set up a college fund for Tad's baby, but Tad wants to provide for him. He says that maybe he will come to me for money somewhere down the road if they hit a bumpy spot, but for now they're all right.

My parents are excited about the money. I booked them a cruise for their wedding anniversary, which is coming up in March.

The magazine is running well. Suzanne and I are great friends, having bonded even more over both of us being jilted by the world's biggest jerk. Suzanne plans to move from her tiny apartment into a condo that has more room for Marcus to grow.

I can't stop thinking about Josh. I keep the pen he gave me in my desk drawer and take it out to look at quite often. It sits next to an envelope containing a rose I pressed from the last bunch he gave me. I'm not depressed, really, just very, very sad.

Despite my best efforts not to, my heart leaps every time I get a text, hoping its Josh.

Today is especially difficult. It's Valentine's Day. I ordered heart-shaped cookies with their names printed on them for the employees, and Suzanne decorated the place with hearts. But I'm just going through the motions. There are no roses from Josh, nor do I expect any.

He had been hurt by people before, and he had finally learned to trust again. Then I hurt him more.

That breaks my heart.

I'm sitting at my desk mulling over my March letter from the editor. March is about inner beauty. I'm trying to decide what to write about, but the fact is, nothing is coming to mind.

Suzanne appears at my door. She is holding an envelope in her hand.

"Read this," she says simply and hands it to me.

I look at the envelope. It's blank. There's no writing on it.

"What is it?" I ask.

"A letter to the editor."

I open it and pull it out. It's typed, and there's no signature.

Dear Editor,

I am a single man who read the February issue of your magazine. I had the world's greatest girlfriend, someone special who appeared in my life one day when I wasn't paying attention and who stole my heart like no one else ever has. Her smile radiates warmth, her eyes dance when she's happy, and she has a heart of gold.

I'm afraid I did some stupid things and made some bad choices, and I need her to forgive me.

You see, I kept telling her how wonderful and special she was. Yet, when she made a mistake, I led her to believe that she couldn't be forgiven, that she wasn't good enough. After all I said and did to show her I loved her, in the end what it all boiled down to was that I was expecting her to be perfect. And she isn't. Nobody is.

Without her, I haven't been able to eat or sleep. It's like a part of me is missing. I want her back.

I love her, and I believe she loves me. You said that Love Forgives. I am hoping that she can find it in her heart to forgive me.

What do I have to do to earn her back?

There's no signature. It's a very touching letter, but how do I find the man who wrote it?

"Who wrote this?" I ask.

I look up. Suzanne is smiling. As she steps aside, there's Josh, standing just outside the door. My heart leaps in my chest, and it's all I can do not to get up and throw myself into his arms.

"May I come in?" he says, all sheepish and cute.

"Yes." My breath leaves me.

"I see you read my letter to the editor."

"Yes." I want to say more, but I can't.

Josh has tears in his eyes. "Forgive me," he says.

"Forgive me too." I'm crying now.

Then I do get up, run around my desk, and throw myself into Josh's arms. It feels so good to be back in his embrace, and we kiss and kiss.

"I've been so stupid," he says.

"No, I was. I am."

We both apologize again and kiss some more.

"It doesn't matter. All that matters is that we're together," Josh says.

"Yes," I say and bury my face in his neck. He smells so good, and he's so warm and comforting.

Suzanne has left the room and closed the door behind her. We're alone, Josh and I. Together. Right where we need to be.

It turns out that Suzanne took our February issue of *Good Enough* to Josh's workplace and asked him to read the letter from the editor. She said he looked horrible when she first saw him, all down and depressed, and his colleagues were worried about him.

She said she did it for the both Josh and me.

I love that girl.

Chapter Twenty-Three

We have Easter dinner at my parents' house, following church. As I'm sitting on the couch afterwards, cuddled in Josh's arm, I'm only half-listening to Josh and Tad happily talking about construction and building projects they worked on in the past and what they're doing now. They're getting along great. I'm just so happy and a bit sleepy from dinner.

Mom and Dad are getting ready to leave on their cruise next week. Mom has already packed, and Dad bought himself a sun hat and is talking to Suzanne about how hard it is to find sunscreen in Michigan when there's still snow on the ground. We invited Suzanne to church and to Easter dinner because she has no place else to go. We invited Harlan too, and he's sitting on a chair across from me, reading the paper. He looks so different from when I first met him. He's clean-shaven, sober, and dressed up for Easter Sunday with a shirt and tie.

My eyes travel to the coffee table, where this month's issue of *Good Enough* is resting. The cover design is amazing, as usual. It's a photo of a woman with her hair pulled back and no makeup on. She's wearing a simple cotton dress and has a bouquet of wildflowers in her hand. She's beautiful. She's simple. She's real.

The theme is "Inner Beauty."

I pick it up and turn to the Editor's Letter. I had help writing this one. I decide to re-read it again.

Inner Beauty

A man's head can be turned by a woman for many reasons. First, of course, is outer appearance. We appreciate the things you do to appeal to us, to try to attract us, even if we don't mention it. We also notice things we probably shouldn't, especially if our significant other is watching us!

But a man's head can be turned by a woman for other reasons too, and it's these reasons that will most likely keep him around for the long run.

I appreciate quality of character in a person. It took me a while to figure out what that meant. At first, I thought that meant integrity, unfailing honesty, and kindness. But then the woman I love lied to me, and I took that one lie to mean she was flawed. What I didn't see was the quality of character in her that had attracted me to her in the first place. She did things she never told others about, like pay her neighbor's bills, help a child in need, and support a man when he was down. She did these things without even thinking about it, because this was part of her character.

She listens to me when I talk. Really listens. And she loves others.

She's beautiful too. She's beautiful when she's dressed up and has her makeup on, of course, but she's also beautiful when she's natural, with her hair in a ponytail under a baseball cap, when she's not trying. It's her smile that lights up her face, and the sparkle of her eyes that catches my breath.

These qualities are what a man looks for in a woman, but I imagine they are what an employer might look for as well, or a friend, or a child. We can't turn back time to erase wrinkles, take back angry words, or pass failed tests. But we can focus on our character and move forward into a better us by using what we already have. Inside every one of us are kindness, goodness, integrity, and beauty. All we have to do is embrace them.

I love my woman. She's the embodiment of all of these things, and she accepts me with all my flaws and positive traits as well. She thinks I'm good enough, and that's what really matters.

By Guest Editor,

Josh Gray

Josh sees me reading, pulls me closer, and smiles. I close the magazine and lean my head against his chest, listening to Tad talk about his construction and how he'd like to pull Josh in for an upcoming job if he's interested. Upstairs, I hear the baby crying, awake and wanting to nurse. I hear Mom pulling her suitcases out of her closet as she looks for her own sun hat that she put away last spring.

This is my life, and it's good.

Good enough.

Acknowledgments

I would like to thank everybody who helped me with this book's journey:

First of all, I thank God for gifting me with writing, and blessing me with the ability to do it for a living. To Him be the glory.

My husband Duane and my two sons, Zack and Logan, the lights of my life. You keep me laughing and consistently remind me to spend more time with the real people in my life than the fictious. You are my favorite characters in the world. I thank God for you every day.

My parents, Floyd and Judy Millard, for encouraging my creativity all these years and always supporting me in every way imaginable. I love you.

My mother-in-law, Arla Gossiaux, for telling me a long time ago that I should write a romance. Here it is!

My friends in Northfield Writer's Group, Leslie, Xanthe, Pam, Anna, Mike, Tom and Greg. Your constant encouragement, support, and amazing talents have helped this writer stay sane. It doesn't go unsaid that this book wouldn't be here without you. Leslie, you are a cover-designer extraordinaire!

My amazing editor, Erin Wolfe, who made me sound really good, and my awesome formatter, Dallas Hodge, who made it all look pretty.

My friend and fellow writer, Colleen Gleason, for sharing your wisdom about this business and your encouragement.

And last, but not least, to my readers. Thank you for continuing to read what I write, which allows me to write more. I love my job and I will try hard not to let you down.

About the Author

Pamela Gossiaux is a humorist, inspirational speaker, and the author of the books *Why Is There a Lemon in My Fruit Salad? How to Stay Sweet When Life Turns Sour,* and *A Kid at Heart*. While she has never found a winning lottery ticket, she's pretty sure if she did she'd squander it on chocolate and books. She lives in Michigan with her husband, two sons, and three cats. Visit her website at PamelaGossiaux.com.

Other Books by
Pamela Gossiaux

Why is There a Lemon in My Fruit Salad? How to Stay Sweet When Life Turns Sour

"Pamela has a way of reaching the reader right where it counts. We relate because we find bits of ourselves in all of her trials and tribulations. I found myself at once laughing right out loud only to be on the verge of tears a page later."

-Debra Mozurkewich,
Amazon.com Reviewer

A Kid At Heart: Becoming a Child of Our Heavenly Father

"Through entertaining stories and text, Pamela reminds us that the ultimate father is waiting with outstretched arms for us to jump into and climb upon his lap."
-Victoria Lovell, award-winning author of *My Guy in the Sky*

Available at PamelaGossiaux.com

162

CPSIA information can be obtained
at www.ICGtesting.com
Printed in the USA
FSOW01n1925220417
33328FS